'A broad and beautifully worked canvas . . . An imaginative, deeply felt and evocative tale' *Sunday Times*

'A daring, imaginative feat; the world it conjures is at once familiar and strange, and strangely moving. A splendid first novel' John Banville

'A novel written with grace and intelligence yet not over-blown with cumbersome literary pretensions is, these days, a rare delight. Tóibín's talent is amazing – a stunning, and very particular novel' *Washington Post*

'A book of sustained lyrical beauty and power . . . Tóibín has a subtle, painterly eye, the direct gaze and sense of place given to exceptional visual artists. His novel is all the more remarkable for its language, so poetic and so direct, pared down to what belongs and nothing else' *Chicago Tribune*

'*The South* is as accomplished a novel as any writer could envy – there is much more to come'

Mary Leland, *Independent on Sunday*

'Clever, evocative and intelligent' *Irish Times*

'This is a memorable piece of writing, dense, quiet and bare, with a presence that fills the spaces the narrative leaves empty. There is a sense of completeness and self-containment about it, at once dispassionate and committed, that gives it a kind of finality, something dignified and unarguable. It suggests remarkable gifts, and a future' *Financial Times*

The South

COLM TÓIBÍN was born in Ireland in 1955. He is the author of eight novels, most recently *Nora Webster* and *The Testament of Mary*, which was shortlisted for the 2013 Man Booker Prize. His other novels include *Brooklyn*, the 2009 Costa Novel of the Year; *The Master*, which was shortlisted for the 2004 Man Booker Prize and won the *LA Times* Book Prize and the IMPAC Book Award; and *The Blackwater Lightship*, which was shortlisted for the 1999 Booker Prize and the 2001 IMPAC Award. His non-fiction includes *Bad Blood*, *Homage to Barcelona*, *The Sign of the Cross* and *Love in a Dark Time*. He is also the author of two short-story collections, *Mothers and Sons*, which was awarded the inaugural Edge Hill Prize, and *The Empty Family*, which was shortlisted for the 2011 Frank O'Connor International Short Story Award. His work has been translated into more than thirty languages. He lives in Dublin.

Also by Colm Tóibín

FICTION

The Heather Blazing   The Story of the Night
The Blackwater Lightship   The Master
Mothers and Sons   Brooklyn   The Empty Family
The Testament of Mary   Nora Webster

NON-FICTION

Bad Blood: A Walk Along the Irish Border
Homage to Barcelona
The Sign of the Cross: Travels in Catholic Europe
Love in a Dark Time: Gay Lives from Wilde to Almodóvar
Lady Gregory's Toothbrush
All a Novelist Needs: Essays on Henry James
New Ways to Kill Your Mother: Writers and Their Families

PLAYS

Beauty in a Broken Place   Testament

Colm Tóibín

THE SOUTH

With an introduction by Roy Foster

PICADOR CLASSIC

First published 1990 by Serpent's Tail

First published in paperback 1992 by Picador

This Picador Classic edition first published 2015 by Picador
an imprint of Pan Macmillan
20 New Wharf Road, London N1 9RR
Associated companies throughout the world
www.panmacmillan.com

ISBN 978-1-4472-7772-9

Reset 2001

Acknowledgement is made to the Tyrone Guthrie Centre at
Annaghmakerring in Ireland where some of this book was written.

5 7 9 8 6 4

A CIP catalogue record for this book is available from the British Library.

Typeset by Intype Libra Ltd
Printed and bound by CPI Group (UK) Ltd, Croydon, CR0 4YY

Visit **www.picador.com/classic** to read more about all our books
and to buy them. You will also find features, author interviews and
news of any author events, and you can sign up for e-newsletters
so that you're always first to hear about our new releases.

Introduction

The South, twenty-five years on

'She reminded herself that she could leave at any time she wanted.' *The South* is, in more than one sense, a novel about new departures. The freedom which Katherine Proctor asserts is hard-won, and she clings to it; but Colm Tóibín's extraordinary first novel traces the way that actions have consequences, and history lays its hold upon us all. It also announced the arrival of a new novelist with a new style – economical, lapidary, incantatory – and a new kind of Irish novel. Twenty-five years later, in the light of the series of path-breaking works which followed it, it is possible to see how Tóibín's assured debut established hallmarks and themes which have dominated his oeuvre. But it is also clear that his first novel appeared at a time – 1990 – when old moulds were being broken, new voices were about to be heard, and Irish fiction, so long identified with short stories in the Chekhovian mode, was about to be characterized by the emergence of a new range of accomplished and original novelists.

This coincided with the unprecedented expansion of the

Irish economy, and the fast-forward development of Irish social *mores*, now known (and satirized) as the 'Celtic Tiger' phenomenon. As old taboos were challenged, ancient limitations transcended, and unsettling new ideas explored, a new kind of Irish novel began to appear from writers such as Dermot Bolger, Anne Enright, Roddy Doyle, Patrick McCabe, Sebastian Barry and – in the North – Robert MacLiam Wilson and Glenn Patterson: works that were often both stimulated by, and mordantly critical of, key aspects of the new dispensation. Tóibín was well to the fore; and – as with John Banville – he had been marking out uncharted territory for some time, though in journalism rather than fiction.

Thus in *The South*, both author and protagonist were striking out on a new path. The novel is about a painter, and it is written with a painterly eye. The way Katherine works a canvas, the structure of line and the infusion of colour, suggests something of the architecture of a painting by the Irish artists Tony O'Malley or Barrie Cooke. Brought up at an angle to the Irish universe, her upperclass Protestant background, and her repudiation of it, resonates with the world of highly talented and individual Irish women artists in the mid-twentieth century (one thinks of Norah McGuinness, Joan Jameson, Letitia Hamilton, Estella Solomons, Kitty Wilmer O'Brien). The narrative devices of the novel are indirect and implicit: Katherine sees things rather than feels them, and her reactions are often strangely distanced. She is independent, observant, sometimes unashamedly selfish, with the sense of self-preservation necessary for an artist's survival (a quality denied to the Spanish painter she will fall in love with).

The structure of the novel manipulates dramatic changes in theme and locale; it is in some ways a novel of two halves, a construction which Tóibín would explore in later works such as *The Story of the Night*. But it is told with a kind of supercharged restraint, rare in a first novel. From the fierce, silent cinematic scene with which the novel opens (a near-rape on a night train), a powerful sense of drama is built up at key points of the story. Tóibín's un-remittingly laconic and elliptical narrative remorselessly carries us along with Katherine on her strange and in some ways circular journey. And, as the title announces, it is central to the novel that this is a journey south: from the wet Slaney valley in County Wexford to the exoticism of the Barrio Gótico in Barcelona, and then the mountains of Catalonia. But 'the south' not only represents the scorching sun and harsh beauty of Spain; it is also the south of Ireland, de Valera's republic, which Katherine runs away from, like her mother before her. Wexford, and particularly Katherine's (and Tóibín's) town of Enniscorthy, marks the site of the cataclysmic 1798 Rising, as well as committed and often brutal campaigning in the 1919–23 war of independence and civil war, a mere thirty years in the past when Katherine flees.

History matters, and like several of Tóibín's novels, history and memory are closely interwoven in *The South* – and often shown to be not quite the same thing. Both Ireland and Spain harbour a memory of violence, half-hidden trau-mas, and – as Katherine will also find out in Catalonia – the merciless backlash of authoritarian structures in church and state. A muted sense of terror hangs in the air. Katherine is haunted by a recurring nightmare of arson, a family house burned around her by the local Republicans, the sound of wind and fire; Miguel carries the memory of terrible things done in the civil war. In a compelling scene between the two, these are spelled out with insistent power and counterpointed with gestures of physical intimacy.

> He wanted her to know everything – did she understand that he wanted her to know everything? Yes, she told him, she did. They had bombed a policeman's house and they had burnt his wife and children to death. He stopped for a moment and held her. This was more than ten years ago and there was a war on, she must remember that, he whispered. He sighed then, and told her that once they had shot a child who had tried to leave the house. He put his arms around her; there was sweat on his hands.

The section of the book set in the mountain hamlet where Katherine and Miguel find a certain kind of freedom and happiness does not flinch from the squalor and inversions of village life, the smouldering hatreds of Spanish history, and the cruel end of idealistic dreams. And this is the place where Katherine begins to interrogate her own family past, and the Ireland which she thought she knew. 'If you knew anything about the country', her fellow-expatriate Michael Graves retorts, 'you wouldn't ask me why I left.'

Katherine's uncertain and half-realized relationship to Ireland is partly expressed through her relationship with her self-centred but perceptive mother, another runaway wife who abandoned a child: a character brilliantly drawn only through the perceptions of other people, but who emerges fully-fledged. Their relationship explores the kind of half-resentful complicity between women which would recur in later Tóibín novels such as *The Blackwater Lightship* and *Nora Webster*. But it also introduces the family history behind Katherine's flight. Her tentative returns to Ireland and the family she left require confronting a new kind of knowledge. The life her son has built for himself throws her own inherited assumptions into sharp relief; the scenes between them show Tóibín's gift for conveying the undertows of resentment, guilt and withholding that characterize the relationships between parents and children in so many of his fictions.

And when Katherine begins to paint in Wexford, she is half-consciously painting history: a history new to her, of rebellion, colonization, poverty.

She began to work; she started to paint as though she was trying to catch the landscape rolling backwards into history, as though horizon was a time as well as a place. Dusk on the Slaney. Over and over. Dusk on the Slaney and the sense of all dusks that have come and gone in one spot in one country, the time it was painted to stand for all time, with all time's ambiguities.

In the distance the rebels lie bleeding.

In the distance no-one has yet set foot.

In the distance a car is moving.

In the distance the sanatorium at Brownswood in Enniscorthy.

In the distance Enniscorthy Castle squats at the top of a hill.

In the distance is the light and the darkness falling,
the clouds moving, the Blackstairs Mountains above
Bunclody, Mount Leinster, the full moon rising.

'Distanced' though she still is, Katherine now sees what
lies beneath the landscape, past and present. And the last
observation invokes a classic rebel ballad, 'The Rising of
the Moon'.

Much as Katherine learns to lay out the structure, scale
and ideas of a painting before she approaches the canvas,
Tóibín was announcing in *The South* the themes which he
would return to again and again. The coast and river landscape of County Wexford, carrying its powerful freight
of historical memory; the relationships between sons and
mothers; illness, loss, grief; the imbrication of power, class
and religion in Irish life; the significance of music in
unlocking the unsaid (not only Beethoven, but – symbol-
ically for Katherine – Tosca's embrace of a life lived for art
and love in 'Vissi d'arte'). And the building-blocks of the
story told in *The South* would find their way forward into
later fictions. Katherine's and Miguel's story is briefly
referred to in 'A Long Winter', Tóibín's magnificent 2006
novella set in those same Catalonian mountains. The burning by Republicans (including members of Tóibín's family)
of Wexford's Big Houses, including that of 'the Proctors
on the Bunclody Road', would be explored in *The Heather
Blazing*. There is even an anticipation of *The Master* via a
nod to the psychological insights offered by the novels of
Henry James (once again, courtesy of Katherine's mother).
'I am like Chad [in *The Ambassadors*]', Katherine reflects
half-ironically: 'still starry-eyed at the sight of the new.'

The novel was written, often at night, over several years when Tóibín was living the high-pressure life of a journalist, editing the crusading magazine *Magill* in the 1980s; a powerful sense of history and politics runs as a current beneath the story of a woman's search for artistic fulfilment. But *The South* also stands as a remarkable achievement within its own terms: intense, suggestive, profoundly moving. Its authority, swiftness and pace still astonish. Much later, Tóibín would remark that reading a certain kind of poetry taught him that 'in a plain statement, you can bury emotion'. The deceptive simplicity and lucidity of the writing in *The South*, widely acclaimed when it was published, buries many things; the manner in which they are revealed shows, already, the hand of a master.

ROY FOSTER

FOR

CATRIONA CROWE

PART ONE

Katherine Proctor

24 October 1950, Barcelona

Night is coming down and there is a hum of noise from the street. I have been here for several weeks. I am grateful that the fat woman who runs this hotel and her little mouse of a husband do not speak English. I remain a mystery to them; they cannot get through to me. The man in the next room – as far as I can understand a word he says – goes to the opera every night and listens to opera on his radio all the time.

They want to know about my husband. They found a man who would act as interpreter for them and he asked me: 'Where is your husband?' The fat woman was there looking at me and the opera man. I told them he was coming soon and I was waiting for him. 'Where is he now?' the man asked me and I told him that my husband was in Paris.

It is difficult for me being on my own and it has been since I left. In the street sometimes I think I am being followed. I try not to move too far away from the hotel. The journey here, however, has been the worst so far.

There are men everywhere watching you. I came in from France to San Sebastian and stayed there in a small hotel looking over the beach and the calm sea.

I was lonely there. I felt bad. In the greyness of the city everything was closed. The streets were deserted every afternoon. The last few holidaymakers were trying at the end of September to wring some satisfaction from the fading sun.

I took the night train to Barcelona. I found what I was looking for in a phrase book: a *coche cama* single, for one person, no sharing. We started at seven in the evening and by eleven I felt tired enough to make up my bed and close the curtains on the small lights which the train flew past.

Barcelona. I did not know what to expect. Bigger than San Sebastian certainly and seedier with a different light coming in from the sea. The Mediterranean. The wide streets bright in the morning. The side streets offering shade. I imagined, but I did not know what to expect. Maybe the sound of the word Bar-ce-lo-na, the sense of pleasure which I caught from the sound of the words, maybe it was the sounds which exerted themselves and held me.

The moment I awoke I knew someone was in the compartment. The train was moving fast. It was still dark so I could see nothing. I stayed still and tried to keep breathing as though I were asleep. There was no question of this being a dream. I knew I was awake; I knew what was happening. This was the night train to Barcelona, some hours before the dawn. This was 1950, late September. I had left my husband. I had left my home. I was not clear about where I was going. I did not wish to be disturbed.

There was a figure standing close to me beside the bed and the door was closed behind him. I had locked the door before I went to bed.

First the hand settled on my wrist for a moment, holding it softly, then harder, then pinning it down. When I stirred and tried to sit up he held my shoulder. He whispered something I didn't understand. I scratched his hands with my nails. I could smell beer on his breath when he put his mouth near mine.

It was a while before I began to shout, I don't know why I waited. He moved back for a moment as though startled but it did not put him off. He was almost on top of me. I tried to scratch his ears and his face. I shouted 'Go away' as loudly as I could, over and over.

I was almost free of him and standing on the floor in my nightdress but he still had a firm grip on my wrist. From his voice I could tell that he was thirty, maybe forty, but no more than that. I was still shouting 'Go away' and I could sense that he was becoming afraid, and that scared me even more because I was worried about what he would do to me before he left – that he would try to hit me or hurt me.

I managed to open the door with my free hand. He tried to pull me back in but I shouted out into the corridor. He let me go and I ran down the corridor. I don't know how but I was still calm enough and clear enough in my mind to remember where the toilet was and I went in and locked the door.

He did not take anything from the compartment. I

must have been calm and clear-headed because I checked that immediately; everything was there. He had hurt my wrist and later I would find a bruise on my shoulder which would take a week or two to disappear. I locked the door again by turning the dangling clasp around into its metal holder. It was easy to see how a piece of cardboard or wood or even a nail file held from outside could have pushed the little clasp right around again and unlocked the door. Still, I locked it and I left it locked.

For a week I felt as though I had jumped through glass, as though every bit of me had been cut or broken or beaten. I walked in a daze through Barcelona in the early morning: the shops pulling up their steel shutters to start the day, children going to school. I noticed the grey blue light softening the stone. I came to a corner, this corner, the corner I am looking out on to now, and I saw a fat woman with tightly permed black hair looking down at me from a balcony. The sign said *pensión* and I shouted up at her and pointed to my luggage. She made a sign with her hands that I was to wait and soon the little mouse, her husband, scuttled down and carried my suitcase up to the first floor. When I gave her my passport she showed me into this room.

For days I stayed in bed marking the time by the sound of the steel shutters of the shops in the street being pulled up and down. First at eight, half eight, nine. That was the morning. Then at one, half one, two, then a few hours later when the siesta was over when it was time for me to get up and even then I was wrecked, pummelled. Even then I only wanted to lie there.

I found a bar just down the street and as the light

began to give, at six o'clock or so, I would go there and have a huge milky coffee and a sandwich made of rough bread and ham or tuna fish. I have to point my finger at what I want. For those early days I wanted nothing but this walk from here to the café and back.

On my first Sunday there were no shutters opening or closing so I was guided only by the cathedral bells. I got up and walked down to the square for my coffee. The sky was warm blue and the sun gave off a surprising heat for late September in Barcelona.

I was careful not to move too far away from my *pensión*. I knew I would have to steel myself. I had bought a map so I knew that I lived close to the cathedral, in the small cluster of streets just up from the port.

I knew that I would have to push myself. I had bought a white cotton dress and a white cotton jacket and a red hat. I was wearing them for the first time. I would have to stop being afraid. I would have to make a decision to go into bars, cafés, restaurants. I would have to be brave. I would have to do as I pleased.

I knew too that there was nothing seriously wrong with me and that I would be all right. I knew that the panic caused by a man I didn't know coming into my compartment in the middle of the night had left a small mark like the bruise on my shoulder which was fading.

The bar was busy this Sunday morning and the square outside was bright, as though specially lit for Sunday. There were paintings on display all around the centre of the square. I was curious. I had been thinking for days about paint; I had avoided letting anything form in my mind. I just knew that I wanted to use paint here. I had known this feeling before and it had always led to intense disappointment and bitter regret. I was having dreams of paint.

I am absorbed in myself most of the time. Sometimes I don't see things around me. I think about myself all the time. What I'm going to do now; how in God's name I'm going to survive.

Plans and fantasies take up most of my waking time. I have all day to think about the future, to plot it out, to dream it, to imagine everything.

The past has happened: it is grey and empty like the narrow streets of San Sebastian at four in the afternoon with the shops all closed and their shutters pulled down. The future is wide open.

I did not go to look at the paintings in the square that day. I felt too well-dressed, too conspicuous. I turned instead into the bar and ordered a coffee. The waiter brought it over to me and I asked for a croissant, but he didn't understand and I had to go up to the bar and point at what I wanted. I had already noticed the man who was standing at the bar. He was wearing a red pullover and brown corduroy trousers; his shirt was open at the neck.

I noticed that every so often he would glance over at me. There was a manic look about him. His dark eyes were close together and his mouth was wide. His teeth were perfect. I noticed he was clean shaven. I looked away. I was not wary of him or afraid. He did not seem like the sort who would follow you in the street. When I looked again he was leaving. He turned and glanced back for a moment and smiled when he found that I was watching.

I walked out into the Plaza del Pino, into the mild heat of midday, and looked at the paintings. The man who had been watching me in the bar was sitting on the ground but when he saw me coming he stood up and put his hands in his pockets. There was a woman, a small dark woman with long hair who was standing behind the easel; she was also selling jewellery. He seemed to be with her. I wasn't sure about this. I nodded my head and smiled at her as I passed by. She said something, it sounded like a greeting, but I didn't understand.

That night I found the real Barcelona for the first time. I had dinner in the Hotel Colón opposite the cathedral and afterwards it was dark and I walked up by the church. I had not been this way before. I had not seen this before. The streets were deserted and there were shadows everywhere cast by the lamps which shone from the walls. The stone of these buildings – the churches, the libraries and museums – was solid and thick. There was hardly anything modern: even the electric light from the walls resembled light from a torch. I found it overwhelming.

Eventually, I walked down a narrow passage which I had thought was a cul-de-sac. The air was still warm and when I touched the stone I was shocked at how cold it was. I remember I stood there and I shivered. I was going to turn back but around the corner I could see an archway leading into a square so I kept on.

There was a small fountain in the middle with two trees on either side. The trees had been pruned down to their essentials: gnarled branches which seemed deformed and grotesque like arms and legs with bits chopped off. It was impossible to imagine how they could grow again.

The square was irregular and dimly lit; there seemed to be another narrow passageway at the other side and I made a note that I would go out that way, although I did not know where it would lead. There was a small church on one side, its walls all damaged by what looked like bullet marks or shrapnel marks. I went over to the opposite side and sat on a ledge. I had been in Barcelona for about a week and suddenly I felt as though I had found the place I had been looking for: the sacred core of the world, a deserted square reached by two narrow alleyways, dimly lit, with a fountain, two trees, a church and some church buildings.

I thought of Enniscorthy. I thought of Tom sitting in the draughty house thinking about me, trying to come to some conclusion about me. I thought of what it would be like to be there. I thought of what it would be like to settle down for the night there with the crows and the jackdaws chattering in the bare oak trees near the river.

I thought of the desolation of the place and I stared at this desolation, this desolation of stone, this stunning, broken-down square behind the cathedral of Barcelona and I knew that I was right to be here. I knew I had to be here.

I thought of my mother's garden in London in late August before I left, when I could not make up my mind what to do. The soothing garden with the huge cherry tree and the run-down sheds, the distant light in late afternoon, the grey flagstones of the garden path, the rickety bird-table, the faint sound of London traffic, the shadows.

My mother told me I was preoccupied. It sounded like an accusation.

'Yes, I am preoccupied,' I told her.

'Are you sure you are right to be preoccupied?' Her tone was mocking and annoyed.

'Did you ever regret leaving my father?'

'No, I did not.'

'Did you never feel guilty?'

'I felt nothing except relief.'

'Even when he died, did you not feel bad?'

'Your father was a nice man.'

'What do you think I should do?'

'Go, go.'

'What about Richard? He's only ten.'

'His father can look after him. He'll be all right.'

'What will I do?'

'Go away somewhere. Spain. I told you, I'll get you the visa. I know someone in the embassy. I'll give you money.'

'Go away somewhere? What do you mean, go away somewhere?'

'Abandon ship.'

'I'm thinking of leaving my husband,' I suddenly said to her. She looked at me sharply.

'Yes, I know. I understand that that is what we are talking about.'

I was thinking. I did not notice the figure at the other side of the square that night. When I saw him I was startled for a moment and considered which way I should run if it should happen that I would need to run. I had thought I was on my own. When he moved from the doorway where he had been sitting and walked towards the fountain I knew who he was. I recognised him by the red pullover. He did not look over until I stood up to leave.

It is late now and I must soon go to eat before the restaurants close. I spend all day doing nothing. I have taken the armchair from the corner of the room and moved it up to the window. I spend hours looking on to the house opposite, looking down on to the street. Nothing happens. After my dinner I drink a brandy with coffee and I am always slightly drunk when I wander back into the Barrio Gótico. And always I light a cigarette in Plaza San Felipe Neri and sit down on the same ledge as I sat on that first night, look around at the square and think about how I am going to manage this.

I have tried to write to Tom. I have tried to say that I want to get away for a while and maybe I will see him soon. That is not what I want to say. I want to say that I am starting my life now. This is not my second chance; this is my first chance. I want to say that I did not choose what I did before, I am not responsible for what I did before. I want to tell him that I have left him. My son is withdrawn from me, my son will look after himself. There is nothing more I can do for him. No matter how guilty I feel I must look after myself.

I am in Barcelona now. I sleep late in the mornings. If I want to sleep in the afternoon I will take some wine at lunch and I will descend into a heavy sleep with vivid dreams which mix up where I am with where I have come from, the stream at Newtownbarry with the fountain in Plaza San Felipe Neri with the Market Square in Enniscorthy. I wake after an hour, maybe two hours, and I feel numbed by the sleep. I sit and brood. I sit and imagine until the light starts to go and then I make my way down the corridor and I shower in cold water. I go and eat and I come back here. Through the walls I have the opera man and his operas in the next room.

I wrote to my mother and gave the address of the *pensión*; this was where money was to be sent. I need more money soon. I did not explain why I am here, what I am doing here, how long I am going to stay; I told my mother nothing. Her reply, when it came, was as brief as her original letter. The money would come through a local bank. Your husband is frantic, he has no idea what you are doing. All my love. There was no mention of Richard; she knew that I had put him out of my mind.

A few weeks ago I tried to take a different route to the Hotel Colón where I was going to have my dinner. I was not in a hurry so when I saw a restaurant and heard a loud murmur of voices inside I stopped and looked. The place looked dingy, perhaps even dirty, but it was full of people drinking at the bar and waiters trying to get by them to the restaurant which was at the back. I ventured in. I suppose I was attracted by the people. I indicated to the waiter and he took it that I wanted a table for one. We both looked around and there seemed to be no free table so I was just going to leave and come back later, or maybe come back some other night, when a couple stood up having paid the bill and the waiter took me to their table. The menu was written in chalk on a blackboard and it was unclear. I had a phrase book which listed items on a menu. I was checking through the book to see if I could find any words on the blackboard when I spotted him.

He was with a number of people at a long table opposite mine; most of them were men but there were also a few young women. He was wearing a light grey suit and an open-necked white shirt. He had his back to me, but at intervals he glanced around. His companions were young, though some were not young enough to be students; they were young enough to laugh at most of what was said. I looked for the woman who had been selling jewellery in the square but she was not there.

At first, I remember, Tom was afraid to let me see him naked. He undressed by sitting on the bed and slipping on his pyjamas. When he turned out the light he would lean away from me in the bed and we made love only when the heat of each other in the same bed brought us together. But even then he was nervous when I touched him. He wanted to lie beside me for a long time holding me with his head buried in my shoulder and neck. He would lie still. Sometimes I thought that he was asleep and I would reach down and touch his penis and it would be hard and waiting. He would gasp for a moment and move his hands along my body. Almost as soon as he was inside me he would ejaculate, crying to himself, whining almost and then he would want to turn and sleep.

It is October in Barcelona. I continue to explore and find new places; days fill up. I change habits. I now have breakfast in Calle Petritxol which winds out of Plaza del

Pino. There are several little cafés that specialise in coffee, chocolate, little sandwiches and pastries. I go to the same one every day at the same time; they know me now and smile at me when I come in.

At first I did not know if they were open on Sundays. As I walked down to find out I passed through Plaza del Pino and found once more the paintings on sale in the middle of the square. I was thinking of him. The crowds were coming out of mass in the church of Santa María del Pino as I walked by. The café was open but all the places near the door were taken so I had to go and sit at the back. As the waiter led me down to a vacant table, I saw him fix his eyes on me. I had not expected to see him here. He was paler than I remembered, but his eyes were the same and his lips. He looked at me as though I were coming to join them at the table. When I sat down he did not look away. His companion was older, more sallow than he, almost unhealthy looking. His face was thin. He was wearing a bow-tie. They continued talking and when they stood up to leave they both smiled at me. He did not look behind as he left.

I went out onto the Ramblas and walked up to Plaza Cataluña and then back down towards the cathedral. I stopped and tried to think for a moment. I tried to work out what I was doing as I walked back towards the paintings in Plaza del Pino. The small woman was there again and he was standing behind her. I walked around looking at the paintings until I came to them. I stopped and the woman spoke to me.

'English? American?' she said.

'English,' I said. He was watching me.

'Tourist?' she asked. I smiled and shrugged.

'You like Barcelona?'

I nodded. The man spoke to her for a while and then they both turned and looked at me.

'You live here in the Barrio Gótico?' she asked.

'I live in Calle del Pino,' I replied.

'You live in *pensión*?'

'Yes.'

'You have family here?'

'No.'

'Work?'

'No.'

'What is your name?'

'Katherine.'

'I am Rosa. Do you like paintings?'

'Yes,' I hesitated, 'yes, sometimes.'

They spoke among themselves and I wondered if I should leave. I wondered if I should walk away.

'He want to paint you, this man,' she said.

I smiled and shook my head.

'No, I don't want to.' She translated for him. 'Is he your husband?' I asked her.

'No.' He looked at me and made a sign as though he had a brush in his hand and painted at his face. He began to nod in assent. I shook my head.

'Why not?' the woman asked. I didn't reply. I pointed to a painting of boats on a beach on the easel beside us.

'Is that his?'

'No,' she said. When she told him what I had asked he laughed.

'He is good painter,' she said and he nodded in agreement.

'I must go,' I said.

In the week that followed I thought I saw him several times on the street. Yet when I did see the painter one day as I was walking towards the market I was startled. He was coming out of a doorway on Puertaferrisa. His lip curled up as though he were amused to meet me by accident in such a way.

'*Bonjour,*' he said.

'Good morning.'

He said something I did not understand. He laughed for a moment and then he pointed at my face and waved an imaginary brush in the air. He kept saying '*si*' and nodding his head. He held my hand for a second in the street.

'I must go. *Je dois aller,*' I said.

'*Non, non,*' he said.

He was insistent, and I wanted to get away. He wanted to know where I lived. I pointed to the *pensión* on the corner. If he called there or disturbed me I could move. There was a *pensión* on every corner.

Yet I became worried that he would call and create a fuss and was relieved when he did not. He simply arrived one day with Rosa and they asked me to come and see their studio. They were eager and friendly. The landlady's face darkened when Rosa spoke in English. I said I would go with them some other day.

'Tomorrow?' she said.

'Yes, that's fine.'

They come again the next day and I went with them

around the corner to Calle Puertaferrisa. It sounds funny but I did not feel nervous about going up the stairs of a house I had never been in before, the same house from which I had seen him coming the other day. After a few flights of stairs he pushed open a door and we went into a huge, long room with large windows at either end and a glass roof. There were easels and paints everywhere. A few people, mostly young women, were sitting on stools, painting from a photograph of a street. The man I had noticed in the café on Sunday was standing behind the easels demonstrating something to one of the students. He looked at us for a minute and then continued what he was doing. The other man looked at me and pointed to himself.

'*Yo, Miguel*,' he said. 'Miguel,' he repeated it.

'*Y tú?*' he asked, pointing at me.

'Katherine,' I said.

'Katherine,' he tried to repeat it.

'Me Tarzan,' I said and he wanted me to say it again but I did not feel able to explain.

'Is this a school?' I asked Rosa.

'Yes, it is a college for painters.'

'I paint,' I said. 'Can I join the college?'

'You must ask Ramon,' she said. She pointed at the sallow man who had been in the café.

'You ask him for me,' I said.

I watched her walk up to where he was standing. The man who had introduced himself as Miguel approached me and when the sallow man glanced down again he could see us both standing together. Eventually, Rosa came over to me.

'Can you come back in a week? He will talk to you then.'

'Will he take me then?' I asked. 'Tell him I can draw.'

'I am not sure,' she said. 'He does not know. You must return next week.'

The cathedral has just rung midnight and there are no more shutters to be pulled down. The day is over. Tomorrow I will go back to the grammar book I bought. Tomorrow I will learn more verbs. But tonight there is no place for me in this city except here in this dingy bedroom in this small hotel. Until the morning no grammar will be of any use to me. Sleep my husband, sleep easy. I will not be back. My son is asleep in Ireland and I will not be back. I will settle into bed. I will sleep. I will not be back. I will think about the future until I fall asleep.

Barcelona

She had forgotten about them now, they came in dreams sometimes and melted into other dreams. She was away. She opened the small window in the bedroom and looked down on Berga. A cold spring morning in the foothills of the Pyrenees. Dead silence. She lit a cigarette and rested her elbows on the window ledge. Mist was still clinging over the town and there was a faint hint of ice in the air.

She was naked and she was aware that if he woke he would see her. She looked around at him, his face angelic in sleep, all malice and amusement gone, all the life taken out of him.

The town had been alive all night. The crowds had come from the villages around; people had come too from Barcelona, from Lérida, from Gerona. Miguel had insisted on taking an early bus from Barcelona and staking his claim on this bed in the back room of his friend's flat. He was given a key to the room, which he locked before they went down into Berga for lunch. He told her to eat as much as she could because there would be no time to eat later. The rest of the day would be spent drinking and shouting, he said, and he looked both words up in her pocket Spanish-English dictionary to make sure she understood. Drinking and shouting.

Miguel met several friends for lunch and they spoke intensely throughout. Katherine tried to follow what they were saying with little success. They spoke in Catalan; for months she had been learning Spanish. Occasionally one of them spoke to her in Spanish but in general they were too involved in their conversation to pay her any attention.

This was Corpus Christi – the opening day of the Patum de Berga. At ten o'clock in the main square the drums would roll and the fireworks would bang in the sky and then the huge giants would walk the streets and the people would try to get as close to them as they could.

Now in the morning the mist was clearing and she could see the few tents pitched on the meadow beside the small river to the north of the town. She stubbed the cigarette out on the window sill and closed the window against the cold morning.

The bed was a mattress on the floor. As she pulled the blankets up and edged her way back into bed, Miguel opened his eyes, closed them again and smiled. He kissed her on the mouth. When he stood up and stretched she lay back and watched him: his straight, thin white back and the rough hair on his legs.

He was cold when he came back from the toilet and they huddled against one another in bed, shuddering at the cold. She gasped when he put his cold hands on her back. For a moment she managed to rest the sole of one foot against his stomach and he cried out and pushed her away.

'Good morning,' he said, trying to mimic her English.

His breath tasted of garlic when he kissed her. He held his face against hers and stared at her, trying to outstare her. He lay on his back and pulled her on top of him with his face buried in her breasts.

He waited a long time before he came into her and when he finished he wanted, as always, to sleep for a while holding her in his arms, keeping her as close to him as he could. Sometimes he would sleep for just five or ten minutes; he would doze and wake again and want to talk to her; sometimes she would not let him know that she didn't understand much of what he said. It was taking her a long time to learn the language.

Jordi owned the flat; Katherine had met him before. His studio was on the floor above with two windows looking down on Berga. She spent the first morning after the Patum watching Jordi paint. The canvases were about three feet in length and a foot across. He had finished six of them which he ranged against the wall for her. All of the canvases had been first painted a bright, almost luminous white. In two of them, this white covered most of the finished surface; in one of these, there was a half moon in black on the white and very thinly towards the bottom of the canvas a worked-over mass in red, blue and pink. She was impressed by the subtlety in the painting, although she still couldn't understand what he was trying to do. She looked at another canvas: the white, faintly luminous background and on the right a number of black lines forming oblique cruciform shapes; nothing else.

The other four paintings were warmer, but still stark. Thick black lines divided squares of colour from one another. Sometimes the paint had been left so thin that it shimmered in the black surroundings. There was a painting of a mountain, brown, black, dark green with scalpel or knife marks incising the canvas and a flat blue sky behind. In the bottom corner were two people, about one inch high, painted like cut-out figures. They seemed to be embracing.

Jordi told her that the paintings had been commissioned by the monks in the abbey of Montserrat. They were the stations of the cross: the fourteen images which represent the closing scenes of the passion of Christ.

They stood looking at the work: the black and white painting, he told her, was the crucifixion; the painting with the half moon and the shapes at the bottom of the canvas was Christ's descent from the cross, the deposition; the three paintings of shimmering colours and black lines were the three times Jesus fell on his way up the hill of Calvary, and the painting of the mountain with the cut-out figures was of his meeting with Mary.

She walked down into Berga to meet Miguel. He was sitting on his own at the bar with a full glass of beer. When they had moved into the restaurant and were looking at the menu Katherine explained to him what Jordi had told her about the paintings of the stations of the cross. He laughed. He put the palm of his hand towards her and rubbed his thumb against his fingers; his face took on a miserly expression. He laughed again. She told him she didn't understand.

'Money,' he said, 'Jordi does it for the money.' He went on to say that Jordi had more interest in the Patum de Berga than he had in the via dolorosa. He just needed the money and the monks were willing to pay. She told him she didn't believe him.

They had pasta and a bottle of rich red wine. Opposite them was a thin man in his thirties whose hair was prematurely grey. His skin was almost yellow; he looked as though he was recovering from some disease. From time to time his eyes darted across the table at them and he paid great attention to the discussion on the stations of the cross. His wine had come in a *porrón* but he didn't hold the spout in the air and let the wine jet into his mouth, as the others did. He poured the wine into his glass from the neck of the *porrón*. She noticed that his eyes were green.

Miguel wanted to talk to her about the future. After his exhibition in Barcelona they would go away together and live in the mountains, north of here, higher up. By that time she would speak Spanish perfectly and could start to learn Catalan.

She was embarrassed by the loudness of his voice and by the vehemence of his tone. They had not discussed money. He did not know that her mother sent her money at intervals. She was unsure what he lived on. There were other things about him she was unsure of; she had no context in which to place him. It was easier to be with him from one day to the next without having to make a grand decision to go and live in the mountains with him.

They went to a bar further along the street and had coffee at a table outside. Miguel ordered a sweet purple drink he called *paxaran*. After two of these and two coffees she felt drunk and tired and she urged him to come back with her to the flat.

★

As soon as they went into the room she took off her clothes. She stood in the middle of the room while he made the bed and smoothed out the sheets. He took off his jacket and shirt and when he was naked he came over and put his arms around her and she could feel his heart beating fast. She could taste the alcohol and the coffee from his mouth as though it were an integral part of him like the pattern of black hairs on his chest. When they were in bed he lay on top of her and his hands held her head; all his energy came from his mouth and tongue. Sometimes he kept his mouth closed and kissed her on the lips. He had left the packet of condoms on the floor beside the mattress; he rolled the rubber down on his penis and she held it and guided it into her. As he moved it in and out she could feel the effortless throb of orgasm come on. He kept his two hands under her as she gasped and he tried to get his penis further and further in. He started to ejaculate and together they held it for as long as they could.

It was twilight. She had turned her back to him before they fell asleep and he lay cupped around her. As soon as she moved he awoke. They were both warm and sweaty in the bed. There was no sound in the house. She turned and kissed him and he put his hands on her breasts;

he held the nipple between his thumb and forefinger; he put his mouth down and kissed it. His penis was hard again. She smiled as she lay on top of him and he put his face against her breasts. He pushed her back and put his tongue between her legs. When he came into her he did not use the rubber but he pulled out when he was ready to ejaculate and sat up. In the dim light she watched the jets of his seed pour on to her stomach.

There was no hot water in the shower and the bathroom was freezing. They stood together under a trickle of ice-cold water and tried to wash themselves. They stood together trying to wash the soap off. Miguel ran back to the bedroom to get towels and clean clothes. By the time they left the house they could see the fireworks and hear the rolling of the drums. The Patum had started.

The drums banged out the same sound: 'Patum! Patum!' The giant figures in the small square towered above everything; the orchestra played fast dance music. The king and queen came first in all their guise of wisdom and solidity and the crowd followed them cheering. The other figures, each of them twelve feet tall, followed on; they, too, seemed majestic and implacable.

Katherine and Miguel moved around the crowd looking for Jordi but they couldn't find him. At one point Katherine noticed the man she had seen earlier in the restaurant, the man with the green eyes and the grey hair. She caught his eye for a second. He looked much more foreign among the crowds of Catalans than at lunchtime.

It was pitch dark and the crowd was gathered around the giants and the drummers in the big square. The fireworks were going off, crackling in the air. The giants' faces seemed as though they might at any moment come to life and frown down at the people of Berga. She wanted to stay and look at them and follow them, but Miguel wanted to go to the bar and buy a *porrón* of a drink he called *mau-mau* so they could wander about the streets for the rest of the night.

'Next year, we can follow the giants,' he said. He looked at her and they walked towards the bar. Next year, she had understood that. *El año que viene.* The year which comes.

They stood in the bar and had a beer. She remembered that he had spoken of the future – next year – as though they had agreed that they would spend the future together. She had not agreed to spend the future with him. She knew nothing about him. What he had told her she had no way of verifying. She went over in her mind again what he had told her. He would soon be thirty-five. He was born in a town called Reus in the province of Tarragona. He had told her he had not married and she had no evidence to the contrary. He had been put in prison for a short while after the civil war – his family was Republican and he hated Franco. He had lived in Paris and in Lyons. He had worked as a waiter in Lyons. But for the past ten years he had lived in Barcelona and, as far as she could make out, for most of this time he had painted. He had shown her the catalogues of his shows going back to July 1944. He told her that he had been involved in the civil war.

She wanted to know if she should trust him. Now here in Berga, late at night in a bar, she wanted to know if she could believe him. She thought of approaching

Rosa. She thought of approaching Ramon Rogent, the painter who ran the studio where she went every day. She would give anything to know more about Miguel, but she realised she could not ask, she would have to watch and find out.

She looked around the bar for a moment. The man with the yellow skin and cat-green eyes was staring at her and when she saw him he stood up and came towards her. He had a carrier-bag in his hand. She turned away from him towards the bar and emptied her bottle of beer into the glass. Miguel was still talking to the barman. 'Do you speak English?' the man asked. The accent was Irish. She stiffened, Miguel also looked at the man.

'*Habla español?*' she used the formal third person to ask if he spoke Spanish. She did not want to meet anyone from Ireland. He said that he spoke it but very badly. Miguel joined in and said that they were a pair then who spoke Spanish badly. The man said nothing. They both looked at him, waiting. He looked at both of them, taking them in, almost smiling at them. Miguel offered to buy him a beer and he accepted. After that no one spoke. Katherine stood uncomfortably at the bar, aware that Miguel was ignoring the man. She excused herself and went to the toilet. When she came back he was still there, self-possessed, quiet, watchful. She wanted him to go away.

'*Es irlandés como tú,*' Miguel said. She told him she knew that already. The man listened to her.

'There is no room at the inn,' he said. 'I can find nowhere to stay tonight.' His hair was thick and cut very short like a grey cap around his head and he looked as if he might be short of money. His shoes were old and worn. He suddenly reminded Katherine of someone she might pass on the road while driving into Enniscorthy.

'Do you know anywhere I can stay?' he asked her.

'Ask him,' she pointed to Miguel who was paying for a *porrón* of *mau-mau* at the bar. Very hesitantly the man explained to Miguel that every hotel and *pensión* in Berga was full. Miguel shrugged his shoulders as though there was nothing he could do. Unless you want to come with us, he said.

'Tell him yes I want to come with you,' the man looked at Katherine. 'Tell him my name is Michael Graves. Tell him I am a painter like him.'

'How do you know he is a painter?'

'I heard you talking at lunch.'

'I saw you watching us.'

'I know.'

'My name is Katherine. This is Miguel.' They shook hands. His hands were small and soft, like a child's.

As soon as they went out into the street Miguel started singing but she couldn't understand the words of the songs. When a group of young people came towards them on the small sloping Ramblas which went down from the square, Miguel stopped them. '*Ese galapaguito no tiene madre,*' he said holding Michael Graves in front of him.

They all laughed and Miguel sang the words again: '*No tiene madre, ese galapaguito no tiene madre.*' 'What's a *galapaguito*?' Michael Graves asked. 'I don't know.' Katherine asked Miguel, who laughed and repeated the

lines from the song. '*Ese galapaguito no tiene madre.*' He
pointed once more at Michael Graves and handed him
the *porrón* of *mau-mau*. Michael drank from the neck.
Miguel indignantly insisted on showing him how to drink
from the spout. Again Katherine asked Miguel to explain
galapaguito but he spotted a middle-aged couple and began
to sing for them. The couple laughed.

'I have a dictionary in my bag. How do you spell
galapaguito,' Katherine asked Michael as she flicked
through the tiny book trying to find the word. 'Have it,
have it! It means "tortoise". The song says, "This little
tortoise has no mother." '

'I don't see the joke,' Michael Graves said. By this time
Miguel had his arm around a number of strangers, and
was singing the song again and pointing at Michael. '*No
tiene madre, no tiene madre, no tiene madre.*'

Later they went back to the bar and found Jordi and
a crowd of others sitting at a long table. Miguel ordered
three beers and made everyone push over to allow them
room at the table. He had stopped singing about the
galapaguito, but he told them all that Michael had no
mother and nowhere to sleep and proceeded to give a
long list of all the other things that Michael did not have.
Everybody laughed, except Michael and Katherine who
did not quite understand. Michael looked around the
table at them all; he did not try to join in.

Katherine wanted to leave; the alcohol was having no
effect on her; she was tired. She asked Miguel for the
key. He asked her where she was going. Home, she said.

He pointed at Michael Graves. 'Are you going with
him?' he asked.

31

'No. Give me the keys.'

He took the keys out of his pocket and as he handed them to her he tried to toss her hair. She turned to the Irishman.

'Good night,' she said.

The door of Jordi's studio on the top floor was unlocked. She went in and turned on the light. The paintings were placed about the walls as before: six stations of the cross, all of them oblique and difficult. The two small figures of Christ and Mary embracing. Above them an enormous dark mountain and beyond that the clear, brilliant blue sky.

She went to the window and opened it; the cold night air came in like a shock. She stared down at the few lights left on in the small village of Berga and the utter darkness all around. Small fields and roads in the foothills of the Pyrenees, small holdings in the hills, small towns, Vich, Solsona, Baga, Cardona, Ripoll. The world turning over in the night. The world breathing in.

*

When she awoke in the morning Miguel was naked beside her. On the other side of her at the edge of the mattress there was someone else. Both men were fast asleep. She knew immediately who the other was. The Irishman. She slipped out of bed and put on some clothes before she went down to the bathroom. As soon as she was dressed she went out.

When she came back they were awake but still in bed. Miguel said he was sick, left for the bathroom and came back with a jug of water which he tried to drink. He

32

was still naked. She wanted him to cover himself while the other man was there. The other man, who was still wearing his shirt, turned away from them as if to go back to sleep. She spoke to him:

'Are you going to stay in Berga?'

'No, I'm going back to Barcelona.'

'Do you live in Barcelona?'

'Yes.'

'How are you getting there?'

'I'm getting the bus.'

'So are we.'

'I know. I'm going with you. Your husband asked me to go with you. I hope that's all right.'

'He's not my husband.'

'He told me he was.'

'He is telling you lies. He is not my husband.'

'He says you are Irish,' the man sat up in bed, he looked dreadful, even more yellow and diseased than the previous day. 'You sound English.' Miguel watched them carefully as they talked.

'Do I?' she asked.

'What part of Ireland are you from?'

'I don't want to talk about Ireland.'

'What's your second name, your surname?'

'Proctor, my name is Katherine Proctor.'

'That's a good Protestant name,' he grinned.

'I've forgotten your name.'

'My name is Michael Graves. I had too much to drink with your husband last night.'

'He is not my husband.' She turned to Miguel. '*Miguel, tú no eres mi marido, verdad?*' He looked at Michael Graves, stood up naked and stretched. She wanted to stand in front of him, to shield him. She wanted him to put some clothes on.

When they had dressed they went up to the studio where Jordi was already working. Miguel asked Michael if he understood the word *dinero*.

'Money,' Michael said. Miguel introduced Jordi as Jordi Dinero and made a sign by rubbing his thumb and forefinger together and pointing at Jordi. 'Dinero,' he mocked. He walked around the studio and looked once more at the paintings. He came to the half moon and told Michael that this was a half peseta which Jordi had lost at the Patum last year and which he wanted to recover. He pointed to the painting of the two figures and the mountain and explained that this was to record the day Jordi received some money from his mother. All the paintings for the monks at Montserrat were, he explained, on the theme of *dinero*, which was why the painter called himself Jordi Dinero.

At first Jordi was amused, but as the speech went on he seemed less so and Katherine noted the bitterness in Miguel's tone. Michael Graves did not say anything. Katherine had no idea how they were going to be rid of him.

Jordi waved to them from his window as they went with their bags towards the bus. There was a crowd at the bus station and they had to wait for the second bus. Miguel wanted them to sit along the back seat so he could look out of the back window. Michael Graves asked her again where she was from.

'I'm from Wexford.'

'So am I,' he said, 'what part are you from?'

'Between Newtownbarry and Enniscorthy.'

'Newtownbarry,' he said, 'they don't call it that any more. I'm from Enniscorthy.'

'You haven't been sent to look for me, have you? Tell me if you have.'

'What do you mean?' he asked.

The House

A few weeks before she left Ireland, Katherine sat one afternoon watching the thundery blue light fall over the river and the fields between the house and river. She watched the oppressive sky, sensing the moisture in the air outside, knowing that no matter how intensely she watched this scene, and studied it, and thought about the colours, she would never get it right.

She simplified it; she left out the stillness, the crushed light from the low sky. She banked the clouds in water-colour on the sheet of paper, emphasised their texture, the grey and black and steely white. She stopped and left it there, and turned again to the window.

She noticed a figure walking up the driveway from the road. A woman walking with difficulty, someone she didn't know; someone begging perhaps, or looking for firewood. She looked back at the watercolour to see if she could include the figure of the woman, but the scale was too small, the figure could only be a brushstroke, a fleck.

She became absorbed in her work and forgot about the woman. Later, it was well over an hour later, she remembered when one of the girls from the kitchen came up to tell her that there was a woman at the back door who wanted to see her and wouldn't go away.

'Who is she? Do you know?'

'She's from out on the road.'

'What does she want?'

'She won't say.'

'Tell her I'm busy now.'

The girl hesitated, as though she was going to say something, but then turned and left the room.

The sky hung low over the river. Katherine moved back to the window and studied the scene once more; there was a bed in the corner, and a heavy double wardrobe stood against the wall, but the carpet had been rolled back carelessly, and the walls were covered with her paintings, the fruits of her labour she called them. The room was cluttered and untidy, unlike the rest of the house; the wash-basin was full of jam jars and brushes and half-finished work lay all over the floor.

The rain started gently at first, it came like the sound of wind, and then the clouds burst open and the rain beat against the window, and the sky became dark and the room all shadows. She watched the window, focused her attention on the drops of rain hitting the glass and dripping down; she stayed there until it was time for her to wash and dress and abandon her private world.

Richard was at the table when she came into the kitchen; he had a friend with him, both boys had their copy-books out and were doing their lessons.

'Can we have some orange squash?' he asked as soon as he saw her.

'Not before dinner,' she said as she went to look at what was boiling on the stove.

'Mary,' she called into the pantry, 'could you roast those potatoes a little when they boil?'

Mary came into the kitchen and looked at her nervously, almost suspiciously.

'What a dreadful day,' Katherine said.

'That woman is still out there, ma'am,' Mary said.

'The woman?'

'She's one of the Kennys, ma'am.'

'Has my husband seen her?'

'He wouldn't talk to her.'

'Is she begging?'

'Oh Lord, no, no, she's not, ma'am.'

'Did you not tell her that I'm busy? The boys haven't eaten yet. Is my husband in the drawing room?'

'She'll get her death out there,' Mary said and gestured towards the door.

Katherine saw the woman again the following day, from her window. It was blustery outside, and she was working in her room with crayon and pencil on paper, drawing the bare trees, the birches and larches across the river, against a sky of dense white clouds. Later she would start to paint the scene; in the meantime she would try out the lines and perspectives, the spareness of what was out there.

*

They left her alone in the afternoons; everyone banned except Richard, who sometimes came and watched her, but he would grow bored and mess with the paint and she would have to send him downstairs.

In general, no one disturbed her so she was irritated by a knock on the door a second day running, and annoyed as Mary came into the room.

'She won't go away, ma'am. I can't get her to go away.'

'Do you know what she wants?'

'She won't say anything ma'am, except that she wants to see you.'

She looked out at the sky, then walked over to the window and stood there. 'I don't know who has encouraged her to come here.'

Mary waited at the door, her expression pained and drawn back. There was silence.

'I'll come down,' Katherine said, 'I'll come down presently.'

When she opened the back door the woman's gaze was sharp and hostile. Katherine didn't speak.

'I knew your father well, ma'am, and all before him. We never done any harm here.'

'I'm sorry, I don't understand why you've been waiting to see me.'

One of the workmen on the farm passed by as they spoke, and suddenly Katherine felt embarrassed standing there. He stopped for a moment and watched them, and then passed on.

'I'm afraid you'll have to tell me what you want, I'm busy just now.'

'We'll be ruined now. This is going to ruin us,' the woman said.

'I don't understand.'

*

After dinner, when Richard had gone to bed, she told her husband what she had heard. A block of wood was sizzling in the grate, foam was oozing out and bubbling in the flame; they both sat and looked into the fire.

'She says that we're going to sue them. They have a few fields adjoining ours down near Marshalstown. I know her, I didn't recognise her at first, but I met her years ago. Her family were always very poor.'

'They're a dreadful nuisance,' Tom said. 'Year after year they let cattle stray in. I'm going to stop it now.'

'Surely you've frightened them enough,' she said. 'I think we should drop it now.'

'This time they're going to pay.'

'They're very poor. They always have been, and things are so hard now, aren't they? That cottage has always been full of children.'

'I'm taking them to court anyway,' he said. His voice came to her across the dimly lit room in a dull thud. Suddenly, she hated his voice.

'We can't do that.'

'Why not? We're doing it.'

'They let the cattle stray into the barley. Is that such a problem?'

'They do it every year. They think we're easy prey.'

'They are our neighbours, you know.'

'They're our bad neighbours,' he said.

'The woman was very disturbed. I don't want to go ahead with the case.'

'We're going ahead.'

'Despite my wishes.'

'Yes, although I wasn't aware of them until now.'

'Now you know how I feel.'

'I do.' He moved across the room to the table and came back with a newspaper which he opened and began to read.

She was not asleep when Tom came into their bedroom, she didn't move, yet when he went down the corridor to the bathroom she got up, closed the door, and turned off the light. When he came back, Tom turned on the light again and Katherine lay motionless. He was sitting on the edge of the bed taking off his shirt, when she sat up.

'Did you turn off the light?' he asked.

'Yes, I'm tired, the light keeps me awake.' She could hear him taking off his vest and dropping each shoe on to the floor. He pulled his pyjamas out from under the pillow.

'I want to talk to you again about the Kennys' court case,' she said. He was crossing the room to turn off the light. 'Leave the light on,' she said. She looked up. He was standing in the middle of the room.

'I thought you were tired.'

'I want you to call off the court case.'

'Why?'

'We've always had good relations with our neighbours.'

'That's why they burned you out, I suppose,' he said. He stood in the middle of the room as though he might at any moment move to turn off the light.

'No one from around here did that. The troublemakers came out here from the town,' she said.

'Nobody knows who did it. It could have been anyone.'

'That's all over now. It was years ago. You weren't here then.'

'We could do without some of our neighbours,' he said.

'And they could do without us,' she laughed. He went over to the light.

'Don't turn off the light, Tom. I haven't finished. I want this to stop, do you understand? I'm not sure I've made myself clear. And if my father were alive, he would want it stopped also.'

'It's your land, is that what you're trying to say? I have no right to make decisions, is that what you're trying to say?'

'You don't understand this place,' she said.

'You and your father obviously knew nothing about it either. I'm not sure there's that much to know, beyond the fact that this is our land, and we don't want our neighbours trespassing on it.'

'I don't think that you've ever quite looked at it,' she said.

'I run this place, and I'll make decisions that need to be made.'

'I suggest that you don't drag our neighbours into the courthouse in Enniscorthy. I think that it would be wrong.'

'Don't interfere, Katherine.'

*

The days grew mild and bright, the last respite before winter. She walked along the lane from the back door to the river; the lane was covered in rotting leaves. The house seemed solid and heavy in the light of an autumn afternoon, angular in the softened air. When she saw Tom walking towards her she was afraid for a moment, but as soon as she understood her fear, she felt a hard and insistent resolve.

'Have you sorted it out yet?' she asked as soon as they met.

'Katherine, don't make it all so difficult.' She turned and walked back with him towards the house.

'I'm making nothing difficult,' she said. 'Have you told them to stop the case?'

'No, I have not.'

'I shall, then.'

'Don't make too much of this. You have no reason to.'

That night when he came to bed he brushed against her, and when she turned away he put his arms around her and kissed her neck. She could feel his penis harden against her.

'Don't, Tom, don't,' she said, and moved towards the edge of the bed. He turned from her and said nothing. Soon she knew by his breathing that he had fallen asleep.

The day of the court case drew near and the woman came again to the house, waiting outside the back door for her. Two days in a row she waited there until it grew dark. Katherine continued to work in her room; she was glad of the escape when she drove into the town to collect Richard from school. She sensed the woman's hostile presence on her return, knowing that everybody in the house was aware of the woman also, and why she was waiting.

44

For once she wanted Richard to be with her in her room; she did not mind his questions – nor his clumsiness. She played a game with him, folding a piece of paper and allowing him to draw one half of a figure while she added the other.

When he went up to bed she read him a story, but he said he was bored by it. She told him she would buy him a new book. She felt protective towards him, but he seemed uneasy with her. He turned away from her and said he wanted to sleep. She went downstairs. Tom was in his office, going through accounts.

'That woman came again today,' she said.

'Yes, I saw her off, told her that if I saw her here again I'd call the Guards.'

'Have you made a decision?' she asked.

'The case will be heard on Wednesday. I think we'll win very heavy damages. All the documents have gone to the solicitors.'

'If you go ahead with it, I'm leaving.' She looked down at him as he sat in the circle of light from the desk lamp.

'Don't make threats,' he said without looking up.

'Tell me if you change your mind,' she said and went back to the drawing room where she sat by the fire.

He was gone by the time she woke on Wednesday morning. She found Richard already in the kitchen when she went downstairs, his breakfast finished. He was waiting to be collected for school by a neighbour.

'Do you know where my husband is?' Katherine asked Mary.

'He had business in the town. He's been gone about half an hour.'

'Did he say when he would be back?'

'Not until the evening.' Katherine realised that Mary was aware of the court case that day.

She sat at the kitchen table with Richard until she heard the blast of the horn. Then she went outside with him into the dim morning. She waved as the car drew away. And when she went back into the kitchen, she noticed that Mary was watching her.

'Could you put the immersion on, I'm going to have a bath,' she said.

'I think it should be hot enough now,' Mary said.

Katherine went up to the cold bathroom and, while the bath filled, stripped and examined herself carefully in the full-length mirror they had saved from the old house after the fire. She looked at her breasts and her belly and her neck. She could see no sign that she was thirty-two; it was as though she had been frozen since her marriage, as though her white skin, and the curves of her body had held, waiting for something. He, too, her husband, must have looked at himself in the mirror, and he must have thought how much older he looked, and how he was a stranger to this house, and he must have wondered why she married him.

Oversleeping and the damp air made her tired, and she could not decide what to do. As the morning wore on, she kept on meeting Mary or one of the girls from the kitchen, and she had to stop to consider how to avoid them. She felt imprisoned; if she used the telephone, one of them might listen on the extension. She went to her room at the top of the house and tried to plan how she would leave.

When she saw an Anglia coming up the drive, she recognised the delivery man from the town. She realised how easy it was going to be. She immediately went down to the kitchen and asked him for a lift into the town. Mary watched her quizzically, almost critically.

She would not take any clothes. She would leave with nothing except her passport and some money. Downstairs, she found the keys of the office over the door, she knew where the money was kept and she took what was in the drawer without counting it. Large Irish ten pound notes and some English twenty pound notes.

'I'll have to make a stop or two on the way in,' the delivery man said as he started the car.

'That's fine,' she said.

'I suppose you'll be going to the court,' he said. 'I suppose you'll be going in to see the case. It won't last long now. That's one open and shut case.'

'Them Kennys,' he continued, 'are awful tinkers, you couldn't trust any of them. They'd steal the eyes out of your head if you weren't looking,' he laughed for a moment and repeated it. 'That's what they'd do.'

He turned right off the main road and drove up a lane. 'I won't be long in here,' he said as he came to a stop. Several sheepdogs came running down from the house, barking loudly as he carried a box of groceries toward the small, whitewashed farmhouse.

Now she was trapped here. They might pass Tom on the road. She imagined their eyes meeting, Tom indicating to the delivery man to stop and she having to get out as though she were a prisoner, to go back to the house as though nothing had happened.

47

She waited. The delivery man came out with a middle-aged woman wearing an apron who stood shading her eyes from the sun while the delivery man came over to the car.

'She has the tea on the table now,' he said.

'Sorry?'

'The tea is hot now and the table is set,' he said. 'And she won't take no for an answer.' The woman at the door of the farmhouse looked towards them.

'I'm afraid I've made a mistake coming with you, my husband will be waiting for me. Perhaps I should have explained,' Katherine spoke evenly. He still stood beside the car. She said again: 'Could you tell the woman that I don't have time, thank you?'

The delivery man didn't say anything until they were near the town. 'I'd say it'll be an open and shut case, ma'am.'

'Could you leave me near the hotel, perhaps at the bridge, would that be all right?'

'You're not going up to the court?' He seemed disappointed. He drove across the bridge and left her at the door of the hotel.

She waited in the entrance hall of the hotel until she felt that he had gone. She ventured out then into Templeshcannon and up past the bacon factory towards the railway station. Her mind focused sharply on the possibilities. She would wait here for the next train to Dublin. She would wait for hours if she had to. Tom would never think of coming here to look for her. She could go south to Rosslare. But she didn't know if the ferry still ran, or at what time, and she didn't want to ask in the station. It would be simpler to buy a ticket to Dublin. It was one o'clock; the court would close for lunch, she imagined, and Tom would drive home and find her gone and he might then notice the money missing.

The sign in the station said there would be a train to Dublin at twenty minutes to three. She checked to see if there were any other notices with the times of ferries to England, but there was nothing. She would have to leave it to chance.

The sky was darkening over the river. Katherine went into the waiting room and sat there, wishing the next twenty-four hours away. She imagined them already over, as if by magic. She thought back over the previous twenty-four hours, thought about how long they seemed. She looked at her watch. Only five minutes had passed. She walked out and stood on the platform until a porter came with a trolley of parcels from the office.

She was in time for the train that would take her to the Dun Laoghaire ferry, he told her. She would be in London in the early morning.

The sea was calm that night, the boat half empty. On the train across England she tried to sleep but she had nowhere to rest her head, and each time she dropped off she woke with a start. She could not wait for the night to be over.

She rang her mother's number from a call box at Euston station. The phone was answered immediately, despite the early hour, and the voice was sprightly and alert.

'In London? Wonderful, do come and see me.'

'I was hoping to come now.'

'Come when you please. I'd be delighted to see you,' her mother sounded less than eager. She did not invite her to stay, but rather spoke as though Katherine wanted only to come and have tea with her. In the long nights and in the anxiety of the previous weeks, she had never thought how her mother would receive the news of her arrival.

She caught a taxi to her mother's house. She was no longer tired, but she needed a change of clothes and a bath. The streets were clear in the grey morning, the city was still asleep. Her mother came to the door, dressed as though for some great event.

'Do tell me all about yourself,' she said.

'You're going to have to let me stay here.'

'Have you left him? Oh good, I'm glad you've left him.'

Katherine washed herself and changed her clothes. They sat in a small room overlooking the garden which gathered in what light came from the sun. Her mother returned again and again to the story of the woman coming up the driveway to implore Katherine not to proceed with the court case.

'What a pity she didn't come with you!' her mother laughed. 'A big Irish cow laying siege to you. I'm so glad you've come.'

In the days that followed Katherine began to laugh too.

'What exactly did she sound like?' her mother asked, but Katherine's effort to imitate the woman's accent was so unreal that her mother laughed even more and wanted her to go on doing it.

'You escaped from Ireland just in time,' her mother said, going over once more all the details of the journey.

Katherine made no plans. Each night her mother made a cocktail with vodka and vermouth and told stories about the Blitz, or went out to poker parties, or to the cinema. One night she invited some friends for drinks and poker. They were English women, all of them, in their sixties and seventies, and they drank several cocktails before they settled down to cards.

'It was the game of poker that got us through the war, my dear,' Katherine's mother said to her, as they played the first hand. Later, when her mother left the room the ladies talked among themselves until one of them turned to Katherine and smiled. 'So you're the friend from Ireland then,' she said.

'I suppose I am,' she said. 'I haven't seen my mother for some years.'

'Your mother? Is your mother here as well?'

'This is my mother's house. I'm her daughter.' It suddenly struck her that she had not been introduced to these people as her mother's daughter, nor had she used the word 'mother' in their presence.

'You're her daughter? I didn't know she had any children.'

'Here she is now. Ask her.'

As they stood in the kitchen when the guests had gone, Katherine asked her mother why she had told her friends that she had no children.

'I put all that behind me.'

'It feels funny being written off like that.'

'Yes, like walking out of the cinema, leaving it all behind, the big picture.'

'Don't make jokes.'

'Katherine, don't tell me what to do.'

'Did I ever exist for you?'

'I got out of that place, and I put it behind me. It's what you're going to do, isn't it? Your father wouldn't come. I don't think you've consulted your spouse. Incidentally, he telephoned twice today.'

'Tom?'

'He'll telephone again tomorrow. I told him I had been in touch with you and I would tell you.'

'Tell him I've left,' she said, and turned away.

Barcelona:
A Portrait of Franco

'We should call this exile's corner,' Michael Graves said, as the waiter poured more sherry into his glass. 'We should put a sign up. Do you know the Irish word for exile?'

'Please tell me,' she said.

'*Deoraí.*'

'How very interesting.'

'Maybe so, but do you know what it means?'

'No.'

'*Deor* means a tear and *deoraí* means one who has known tears.'

'I see no deep furrows on your cheeks,' she said.

'That's because, like you, I'm not really an exile, but an émigré. Delighted to get out. A great country to emigrate from is ours. "And after this our exile . . ." ' he began to intone.

'What's that?'

'It's a prayer. "Hail Holy Queen Mother of Mercy, Hail Our Life Our Sweetness and Our Hope, to Thee do we send up our sighs mourning and weeping in this

valley of tears . . ." You say it at the end of the Rosary.
Do you know what the Rosary is?'

'A prayer.'

'Too true. It's a prayer.'

He spoke to her with a mocking ease she had not
come across before; he insisted on a familiarity she still
found disconcerting. Even now as he talked to her and
half jeered her, she could not rule out the possibility that
this Michael Graves might go away and leave them alone,
and that she would greet his departure with mixed feelings. She had become used to his face, yellow and sunken
like an apple left out in the sun. Miguel too had warmed
to him. He liked foreigners, he told her once, adding so
would she, if she had lived in Barcelona for ten years.
She had tried to tell him that there were other foreigners
available should he tire of the ones he was with now, but
he had missed her point.

'How many drinks did you have with Miguel before I
met you this evening?' she asked Michael Graves.

'Five,' he said.

'Five what?'

'Five drinks.'

'What was in them?' she asked.

'Miguel ordered them. Miguel paid for them. I am the
innocent party.'

Miguel's paintings covered the walls. He had been
working hard for weeks finishing off paintings that he
had previously cast aside, trying to recover paintings
he had done years before and beginning new work. These
last weeks he had painted all night in a corner of Ramon
Rogent's studio in Puertaferrisa. His eyes glazed over,

Katherine noticed, when anything except his exhibition was mentioned. She had watched Michael Graves become Miguel's friend and adviser, telling him in broken Spanish what he should do with his paintings, how he should frame them, whether he should varnish them and which he should discard.

At some point in every day Michael Graves would turn up. If he came in the late afternoon he would stay drinking and talking as long as there was company; but sometimes he arrived in the morning and disappeared by lunchtime. He lived in a *pensión* in the Barrio Chino. It was cheap, he said, and he enjoyed the atmosphere. They knew nothing about him: they did not know why he was there, nor how long he intended to stay, nor what he did with his time. His head was full of information from books he had read and people he had met. One day he brought them a pile of his drawings of scenes in the Barrio Chino. All the students were impressed. Ramon Rogent wanted to buy one of them.

That afternoon she took him to one of the bars in the market off the Ramblas. He seemed nervous and overwrought.

'Maybe I shouldn't have brought those drawings in,' he said.

'Everybody thinks they're very good,' Katherine replied.

'I have a basic competence, that's what Rogent liked, the native thing, the thing you're born with. I don't know how much I should charge for the drawings. I need the money.'

'He's not rich.'

'I need to sell more than one of those drawings. I have no money. Otherwise I'd keep them myself.'

'Didn't you have money before you came here?' she asked.

'I did but I spent it. I need a few commissions.'

'Do you want a loan of money?'

'Yes.'

'How much?'

'This much plus a bit more.' He put his *pensión* bill on the table. It was not high.

'I can give you that tomorrow,' she said.

'I need it today. They have my passport in the *pensión* and if they don't get paid today they're going to call the police.'

'Let's go to the bank.'

'I'll give it back to you,' he said. She was surprised at how calm he was.

*

In the week before the exhibition, a small man appeared once a day at Ramon Rogent's studio and took away the paintings that were ready. Rogent and Miguel called him Jordi Gil. Michael Graves, who disliked him, called him Shylock and did imitations of him rubbing his hands gleefully at the sight of money. Michael went to the British Institute and joined the library in order to borrow *The Complete Shakespeare* from which he made Katherine read *The Merchant of Venice*. He cast her in the role of Jessica, Shylock's daughter. 'Sit Jessica,' he would say at any opportunity, 'look how the floor of heaven is thick inlaid with patterns of bright gold.'

Sometimes he bored her. She thought his dislike of Jordi Gil was irrational. She returned to her grammar book and her *pensión* window, to her walks around the Barrio Gótico, her solitary meals in the restaurant in Hotel Colón, her visits to Plaza San Felipe Neri.

The painting classes with Ramon Rogent gave her a focus. She went for a meal or a drink with anyone who was free; but Miguel was preoccupied with his exhibition, he was not preoccupied with her.

The exhibition was important. There would be a big opening in the gallery with colour reproductions in the catalogue. The prices would be high, the gallery was good. Jordi Gil had given Miguel an advance and if enough paintings were sold Miguel said he wanted to go and live in the Pyrenees. She was lying in bed one morning in the room he kept in a friend's flat in Gracia. She thought he had gone out for the day. She lay in the darkened room worried about being pregnant: they had made love during the night without using a contraceptive. They had taken the risk. She would soon have to make a decision about Miguel.

He came back into the room and stood at the foot of the bed with his hands on the iron rail. '*Quieres venir conmigo para vivir en un pueblo del pirineo?*' She translated it to herself in a whisper. *Do you want to come and live with me in a village in the Pyrenees?* She curled up in the bed for a moment and turned her head towards the wall. She let the silence continue. After a while she sat up in bed and looked at him. His hands still clutched the rail.

'*Si*,' she said. His lip curled as though he were amused.

He went out. She reminded herself that she could leave at any time she wanted.

*

Ramon Rogent taught her to use black for delineation as though the paintbrush were a pencil. He taught her to draw the painting first using the black oil paint. From then on the problems were weight and texture. He taught her that light was a form of weight. He showed her how Picasso made painting seem like sculpture, giving each colour a weight in its application, as though it were mass. He showed her reproductions of Matisse and Dufy and illustrated how they had used black paint to draw the lines and then colour to fix the weight and the texture. She came back every day and worked on this.

Rogent was working on a big painting called *The Rocking Chair*, using a model in an elaborate floral dress sitting in a rocking chair with a window open on to a balcony. He showed her the sketches he had made for the painting, how he had planned the same pink to appear on the face and arms of the woman, on a building in the background outside and as dots on the woman's dress. But the force of the painting would arise from the use of black to make lines and shadows. Over and over Rogent worked on the black. He taught her how to use black.

Michael Graves remained uneasy about what she was learning. She should learn to draw with a pencil, he maintained, not to make fake marks with black oil and fake textures with fake colours. He took his sketch book one day when they went to Tibidabo and she spent the afternoon watching him draw Barcelona down below with the sea beyond. He drew with a fluency she had never imagined possible. He was a much better draughtsman than either Miguel or Rogent.

'Where did you learn to draw like that?'

'I always knew. I just practised it and developed it. I worked at it. You should work at it too, instead of learning how to put daubs on canvas.'

'What did you do before you came here?'

'Very little. I was a teacher. I worked in a hospital.'

'What part of Enniscorthy are you from?' She had tried to ask him this before but he had evaded the question. This time he answered freely.

'Do you know Frank Roche's house, Slaney Lodge?'

'Yes, of course I do.'

'There are four houses in a terrace just opposite that. I was born in one of those.'

'They're very small.'

'Yes, to you they would be very small.' He looked at her with his big green eyes. She noted the mockery, the bitterness, the irony. She lit a cigarette.

'Why don't you smoke?' she asked him.

'My lungs,' he said.

'What's wrong with your lungs?'

'They're in bad shape.'

'Why?'

'TB,' he said.

'How long did you have TB?'

'Years.'

'Were you in hospital?'

'I was in hospital.'

'For how long?'

'Have you ever read a book called *The Magic Mountain*?' he asked.

'No,' she said.

'It was like *The Magic Mountain* except more people died. Almost everybody died. I didn't die.'

He held her hand for a moment and moved closer to where she sat on the grass. He rested his head on her shoulder. 'How long did you have TB?' she asked. He didn't answer. Gently he put his hand on her breast and held it there.

'Michael, Michael,' she whispered. He didn't move.

'I want to go,' she said. 'Please don't.' She pulled his hand back and held it. They walked in silence to the tram in the warm afternoon.

*

She expected to see nothing familiar in this strange city so that when she glanced into the gallery and saw Miguel's paintings hung on the walls she was shocked. It was like visiting home for an instant, or like seeing someone's handwriting in a new context. She stopped in the street and it was a full instant before she knew what she was looking at. She had forgotten the frenetic preparations for the exhibition.

When she went in she was disappointed as she knew she would be. She had liked only the academic work she had seen of Miguel's – the still lifes, the portraits. This, she felt, was too surrealist: there were too many images, too many statements. Prison bars turned into snakes, men's arms turned into rifles; there were coffins.

She had heard Miguel's arguments with Rogent about painting and she had observed the difference between them. Rogent talked about colour and form, he talked about beauty, he spoke about using paint almost for its own sake. Miguel believed that paintings should state something, should tell the truth, should be assertive. Miguel admired Goya for his *Third of May*; Ramon admired Goya for his court portraits as well. Their views were so clear-cut and far apart that Katherine had no difficulty understanding them. Nor had she any difficulty siding with Ramon Rogent. She felt this sharply as she moved about the gallery.

*

There had been tension all that week over Miguel's portrait of Franco which he had begun several years before. He disappeared for a day with the canvas and when he came back to Rogent's studio he wouldn't allow anyone to see it. He cleared a space in the corner and worked all night, making sure that no one could catch a glimpse of what he was doing. Katherine understood the tension, knew why the students were standing around and why Rogent was so nervous. Miguel was painting Franco.

Rogent's wife Montserrat was in the studio that night and tried to explain the problem to Katherine further, but she couldn't understand what Montserrat was saying; she just nodded. Eventually, Rosa, who seemed to work as Rogent's assistant, came back and Katherine was able to ask her what the problem was.

'His painting wishes to insult the Franco,' Rosa replied.

'Is that why everyone is so worried?' she asked.

61

'If the police find it he will be arrested.'

'Miguel?'

'Yes, and if the police find it here in the studio of Rogent, they will arrest Rogent also.'

'But is the painting not for the exhibition?' she asked.

'Miguel want it for the exhibition but . . .' Rosa made a sign as if to cut her throat.

In the morning Rogent was still there. A blond stubble stood out on his thin face. Montserrat had gone, but Michael Graves had turned up and was standing beside Miguel at the easel. Only Michael Graves had been allowed to look at the painting. When he saw her he came running down the studio. 'He's a genius, your husband. I know he's not your husband, but he's a genius.'

Rogent wanted to know what was going on. He seemed flustered. Michael Graves shrugged his shoulders as though he couldn't understand. He turned to Katherine. 'The painting, Miguel told me to tell you, is called *The Death of Franco* and it shows Franco dead in a coffin. There's a huge rat eating at him and bits of him are being eaten by worms. It's a great bloody painting. It's terrific.'

'But he can't do that,' she said.

'Why can't he? Of course he can.'

'He'll be arrested.'

'Who'll arrest him?'

'The police.'

'I'll arrest him if he doesn't finish it,' Michael said. 'He's a genius, your husband.'

'This is Spain, there will be problems,' she said.

'Let there be problems, it's about time there were problems,' he replied.

*

When Miguel was too tired to keep working, Michael Graves sat like a lean greyhound guarding the painting. His green eyes fixed on anyone who came into the studio as though he would bite them if they came close. He sat on the chair the wrong way around, his arms resting on the wooden back. When Miguel came back they talked for a while. Michael Graves irritated Katherine; she had no idea how he and Miguel managed to communicate: Miguel spoke no English and Michael's Spanish was rudimentary. They were still talking when Ramon Rogent came back into the studio accompanied by Jordi Gil. Gil immediately shouted something down at Miguel. It sounded like an order; it was in Catalan. Miguel walked up towards him, Katherine noticed that his fists were clenched. He began to shout. Rogent said nothing. He was pale.

Miguel came so close to him that Gil had to move back a few steps. He pointed his finger at him and poked him in the chest. They both shouted in Catalan. Gil kept pointing to the painting at the top of the room. Katherine went over to Rosa and asked her what they were saying.

'Mr Gil say that he not include this painting in the exhibition. Miguel say that this painting must be included,' she said.

Michael Graves came over to Rosa. 'How do you say "coward"?' he asked.

'*Cobarde*,' she said.

'*Cobarde*, sounds logical,' he said. He went over to Gil. '*Cobarde*,' he said.

'*Cobarde*,' he repeated. He hunched down so that he stood as small as Gil and put his face up against his.

'*Cobarde*,' he said again.

Gil's face was red; he looked as if he were going to burst. He spoke quietly to Rogent and then went to the door. Eventually, Miguel and Rogent joined Gil and the three of them went out into the street.

Michael Graves took up his position as guard of the painting again, and Rosa sat in front of him with a pencil and sketch pad and began to draw him guarding the painting. She told them that Rogent was worried that one of the students would go to the police and inform on Miguel. She said it was impossible to tell which side people were on, even Catalan people. Michael Graves said he was going to the police if the painting wasn't in the exhibition. Rosa used different pencils in the sketch to get different effects. Michael Graves seemed pleased about being sketched and sat as motionless as he could, guarding the painting of Franco. 'You'll have to stop behaving like a child,' Katherine said to him.

When Katherine went out to look for them they were not in the gallery nor in any of the cafés along the street. She went into the bar in the Plaza del Pino to have a beer and a sandwich and she found the three of them sitting there. Gil was writing out a list of names. At intervals one of them would call out a name and they would all laugh – sometimes this name would be added to the list, other times not.

Miguel explained to her that he had reached a compromise with Gil. He had agreed not to include the painting in the exhibition if Gil agreed to pay for a separate party the night before the opening at which the painting would be on show. They were preparing a list of those who were to be invited and it was important that no one on the list was a fascist, or a spy, Miguel said.

*

Most of those invited, however, did not turn up. When Gil made a speech, the small audience laughed at the constant interjections by Michael Graves. The painting was unveiled, bottles of champagne were opened and Katherine felt that people were disappointed by the painting, that it did not seem shocking to the few students and artists there.

Jordi Gil filled everyone's glass with champagne. Katherine went over and examined the painting. The face was not right; she would not have recognised the man as Franco, that was the first failure. The sense, however, of something rotting was, she felt, good. The rat was frightening; the tail lingered over the face as the teeth nibbled at the shoulder. Rogent saw her looking at it and came over. He asked her if she liked it. When she said no, she did not, he agreed with her.

She told him she enjoyed the classes and laughed when he said she was his best student. He told her she should try and be serious about it and work hard. They both glanced over at Michael Graves who had his arms around Jordi Gil and was singing a song. Katherine asked Rogent what he thought of Michael Graves's drawings.

'His drawings are marvellous,' he said. Rogent looked

over at him as he sang. 'But he's more interested in life than in painting.' Katherine noticed Miguel watching her from the other side of the room; she smiled at him and he winked back.

*

Enough paintings sold at the real opening the following night for Jordi Gil to be satisfied, for the row to be forgotten. Katherine stood with Michael Graves as the crowd began to thin out. Miguel came over and told them that Gil had given him more money and he had booked a long table in Barceloneta.

The night was warm. They drove in a taxi down to the statue of Columbus from where they could see the ships in the port and then turned left towards the station and then down by the warehouses to Barceloneta. Miguel ordered the taxi to stop before they arrived at the restaurant and they went into a bar on the corner of one of the narrow streets.

Miguel and Michael Graves ordered *absenta* as an aperitif; Katherine had a beer. This was the second night in a row spent drinking and Katherine did not think she could drink much longer. She had hardly touched her beer by the time Michael Graves ordered another round of drinks. She told Michael Graves to stop drinking so fast. Miguel told her to stop talking in English, since he could not understand. Katherine told him in Spanish what she had said and he told her it was her fault, she was drinking too slowly.

In the restaurant the others were waiting. They ordered a paella and white wine. Michael Graves said he wanted red wine; Miguel agreed, said he wanted red wine as well. After the meal they had several brandies each and stayed on at the table when the others left, moving from the restaurant back to the bar they had visited earlier. Katherine was, by now, enjoying the drink but Miguel and Michael Graves had gone too far in drunkenness for her to catch up. By midnight the bar was closing up and they had to leave.

They walked up through Barceloneta to the city, watching out for any bars open along the way. She heard Miguel telling Michael Graves a story about his time in prison; she found it impossible to follow the story. Michael Graves nodded but she doubted he understood. At Via Layetana they found a bar open.

She lost count of the bars they went into. At three in the morning they were close to the Ramblas and Michael Graves said that he hadn't felt so sober in years, he needed more drink. Miguel tried to speak in English and Michael Graves taught him how to say 'I need more drink'. The night was still warm as they walked up the Ramblas towards Plaza Cataluña; the street was being washed down with hoses. A taxi went by. Miguel whistled. When it stopped some distance from them, they ran towards it. Miguel spoke to the driver; he didn't seem to know where he wanted to go and the driver seemed unsure, but after a while the taxi moved off towards Plaza Cataluña and towards the university. Katherine asked Miguel where they were going.

'*Le pedí que nos llere a un bar o a cualquier lugar que no sea bordelo ni tampaco muy caro,*' he said, and she explained to Michael Graves that the taxi driver was taking them to a bar that was neither a brothel nor very expensive. 'Good,' he said. 'I'm glad we're going to a brothel.'

'No,' she told him. 'We're not going to a brothel.'

'Yes, I know. I'm listening. I understood Miguel when he was talking.'

The taxi stopped in a deserted street at the entrance to an underground garage. The taxi driver told Miguel there was a bar in the garage. The taxi drove away and left them there in the dark street staring at the dark empty building. They walked into the garage but there was no sign of a bar, only a small door to the left, possibly a side entrance to the main building. Miguel went to try the handle and then moved back startled, as the door opened and two people came out and went by, towards the street. He put his head through the door, and found a bar, just as the taxi driver had promised. He beckoned the others to follow him.

As soon as they sat down they were handed a menu; the place was half full; loud music was playing. Katherine looked around but could find no other entrance except the one they had just come in. It occurred to Katherine that most of the women looked like prostitutes. Michael Graves proposed they order sandwiches and cold beer. The beer would wake them up, he said. And when the beer was finished he planned to have brandy and coffee.

Miguel began to talk about what to do with the painting of Franco which he had returned to Rogent's studio. He had promised not to leave it there. Michael Graves proposed that they post it to Franco. Or maybe to his wife. 'What is his wife's name?' he asked Miguel, but Miguel was preoccupied trying to attract the waiter's attention. Michael Graves noticed the people in the booth behind, who looked like two businessmen and their girlfriends, and asked: '*La esposa de Franco, cómo se llama?*' They immediately seemed hostile, Katherine realised. She held Michael's wrist and told him to stop.

*

The vague light of the dawn was filling the sky around the port. The Ramblas was deserted. It was five o'clock in the morning. In half an hour the bars in the market would open, but in the meantime there was nowhere for them to go except back to Rogent's studio, there to decide whether to go home or continue drinking. Miguel was still talking about his portrait of Franco and how he wanted to present it to the Modern Art Museum. Michael Graves wanted to take it down immediately and leave it at the gates of the museum.

Katherine was tired but her head was racing after all the double coffees they had ordered in the garage. When Miguel began to wrap the painting in the studio she assumed at first that he was taking it to his flat. Michael Graves asked Miguel whether he was really going to leave it at the gates of the Modern Art Museum. Miguel said no, he was going to leave it in Plaza San Jaime – there it would have more impact – the police building was on one side and the municipal building on the other. He continued wrapping the painting.

'*Pero siempre hay policía por ahí,*' Michael Graves said. Katherine agreed. Miguel said he wanted to lean the painting against the main door of the police building. There wouldn't be any police at five in the morning.

*

They had passed the entrance to the cathedral cloisters when they saw the two policemen coming towards them. Miguel was carrying the painting, Katherine and Michael Graves were walking on either side of him. None of them stopped or even hesitated; they walked straight towards the policemen. Miguel tried to whisper that these were not Guardia Civiles, they were just a local militia, and there was no problem. Katherine thought that there was a problem. The policemen appeared to have agreed somehow to stop them and asked questions. '*Dónde van?*' one asked. Both of the police were middle-aged. '*A coger un taxi,*' Miguel answered. '*Qué es eso?*' one policeman said pointing to the painting, wrapped in brown paper. Miguel replied that it was a painting, that he was a painter and these were two friends from Ireland. The policemen looked at Katherine and at Michael Graves.

All they had to do was ask to see the painting. Even if the figure did not look like Franco, it was obviously military. Katherine suddenly felt cold, as though she wasn't wearing enough clothes. The policemen stood in front of them and looked at them, watched their eyes. The cathedral bell rang half past five. The policemen did not move. Katherine thought about Plaza San Felipe Neri just a few yards away, how peaceful it was, how enclosed.

One of the policemen kept on looking at her. She tried to think of the words of a song, or a poem, something to concentrate on. The other policeman put his foot down on Miguel's toe and pressed down hard. Miguel did not move.

'*Tu eres catalan, verdad?*' he asked.

'*Si*,' Miguel replied. The policeman continued to press on Miguel's foot. His companion continued to stare at Katherine.

> They shall grow not old as we that are left grow old
> Age shall not weary them nor the years condemn
> At the going down of the sun and in the morning
> We shall remember them.

She said the words to herself over and over to keep her mind from what was happening. They could hear the pigeons up in the stone walls of the cathedral and the distant sound of a car, but nothing else. The policeman drew back his foot and stared at Miguel, daring him to move. Then, suddenly, without any apparent consultation, both policemen walked on. Katherine was afraid to look behind, to make sure they had gone. No one spoke. The three of them walked quietly on up the street to the plaza. Miguel was pale. Katherine said she wanted to go home. Miguel said that they should turn down towards Via Layetana.

When they reached the square, they saw that the two huge doors of the police building were closed and there was no guard outside. Katherine knew Miguel well enough to realise that he was tempted for a moment to cross the square and leave the painting there, but he didn't. They turned left instead to Via Layetana and went back towards the studio.

Pallosa

After eight hours on the bus they arrived. Over and over Katherine had asked Miguel if they were nearly there. The bus had turned another bend in the interminable, steep climb and her ears had popped; and a few minutes later Michael Graves had turned round to say that his ears had popped as well.

The air was cold in Llavorsi, even though it was early afternoon. It was as though ice had been added to the air. And there was the sound, a sound which was to become abiding, day after day, the sound of water rushing, falling against rock. Llavorsi was as high as they could go; impossible that there could be anything beyond, she felt.

They rested against a low wall while Miguel went to find the man he hoped would rent him the house. They shivered with the cold.

'We are going to have to buy winter clothes,' Katherine said to Michael Graves.

'It's a wonderful cold,' he said. 'There's no dampness here. It's crisp. It's good for your lungs.'

'Do you know where this house is?'

'I think it's a good distance away from here. Higher up.'

'That means it's going to be even colder.'

'I think it's very remote,' Michael said.

'Are you going to stay?' Katherine asked.

'Until my welcome runs out and then I'll go back to Barcelona.'

'That's a good excuse. When do you expect your welcome to run out?'

'You're very difficult to deal with. I don't know if you understand that. Your husband is much simpler,' he said, and they both laughed as she immediately retorted: 'He's not my husband.'

'What will you do in Barcelona?' she asked.

'I've been promised work as a teacher. I used to be a teacher in Ireland.'

'Why did you leave Ireland?'

'I was sick,' he said. 'I was sick of Ireland,' he laughed.

'Seriously, Michael.'

'Seriously, if you knew anything about the country you wouldn't ask me why I left.'

*

A jeep came around the corner with a local man driving and Miguel in the front seat. The driver didn't move while Miguel got out and opened the doors at the back so they could put their bags in. Between his thumb and forefinger he dangled a ring of keys, several of which were large and rusty. Michael and Katherine sat on facing seats in the back of the jeep. Miguel grinned at them as the jeep started.

The road was narrow. There was a small river down a steep bank and there was a sense everywhere of luxuriant green growth, of the damp earth of the Pyrenees springing into life. Michael Graves knelt on the floor looking out of the window, his elbows resting on the seat. She knelt beside him.

They began to climb again. The road became a dirt track cut into the rock. Down below was a valley of fields and forests. Once they had passed through the first village it seemed once more impossible that there could be any habitation higher up. The jeep was having real difficulty with the track and stalled several times.

She had a real sense now of how high they were: not just because of the cold, but also because of the shape of the rock and the sheer drop into the valley beneath, even the mountains in the distance seemed to be lower down. Michael Graves constantly pointed things out to her: the brown rock of the mountain, the deep blue of the sky, the patches of snow on ridges in the distance, the light green of the pasture and the darker green of the trees that peppered the fields or stood in long rows.

Suddenly Miguel pointed at something just above the jeep and Michael Graves roared: 'Look, it's an eagle,' and caught Katherine's hand in excitement. The eagle hovered; huge, black and grey, holding itself maybe thirty feet out from the track as the jeep turned the corner. Michael Graves and Katherine looked back and saw the eagle hanging like a piece of paper in the high air.

Michael Graves asked Miguel if he had been here before. Miguel answered that he had spent several months in Pallosa, ten years ago. After the civil war.

'*El pueblo está abandonado*,' he said. Now there were only three or four families and about thirty houses, all of them in good repair. Their house had running water but no electricity. '*Es grande la casa que hemos alquilado?*' Katherine asked him. Yes, it was big. He would have to go back down with the driver to collect supplies such as candles, food, blankets and some furniture, and would be back up later. He told them he had paid a year's rent for the house.

He asked her if she was going to stay with him for a year. The driver and Michael Graves listened. She could not answer. She looked out of the window: they were passing through another, smaller village. He repeated the question. She was not sure if he was mocking.

'*Vas a quedarte conmigo un año?*' She looked at him plainly. '*Sí,*' she said.

They were still climbing. The road twisted less and less. Instead of rock now, there was tufted grass to the left and the drop down into the valley on the other side was gentler. It was as though they had come to the end of the earth, the landscape had played itself out, and this was the quiet top of the world.

'*Está muy lejos?*' she asked him and he said no, it was not far, they were almost there. They had now been travelling for over nine hours; the sun was low and mellow in the sky.

The village was sheltered below the summit in a small dip; it stretched out beyond a stone church and a narrow street of houses towards a valley. The houses had been built from the yellow-brown stone of the mountains and the rock behind the village was bare so that it was difficult at first to make out some of the houses. A woman leading cows through the village turned and looked when she saw the jeep and then walked on. The jeep moved slowly behind her. When Katherine asked Miguel which house was theirs, he pointed towards the end of the street.

*

The house looked extremely small with just a door, one window and a balcony. It seemed to be the smallest and shabbiest in the village; some of the others had three and four storeys and huge windows. Inside, however, it was much larger. There was a bedroom with a balcony and a kitchen after that. At the end of the corridor there was a long room with two windows which looked out to the valley. Off that there was a toilet and another bedroom.

They walked through the house without speaking. It was Michael Graves who discovered the long room at the end of the corridor and took her down to look at it. She went into the toilet and pulled the chain. 'It works,' she said. 'The house is wonderful.' She pulled back the shutters on one of the windows and walked out on to the small balcony.

The church lay over to the right. Beyond the long valley were snow-covered mountains; the valley was darkening as evening came down. The small hills to the left were capped by a pine forest. She stood there and gripped the railings. The others had gone back inside. She looked down on the valley, trying to register it carefully as though she was preparing an inventory of each shade in the valley and the hills, as though she wanted to be able, at some time in the future, to remember exactly what this felt like.

She was disturbed by Michael Graves, asking her, 'Have you been upstairs?'

'What? Is there an upstairs?'

'Yes, there's a bedroom up there. Come on, I'll show you.'

He led her to another door off the corridor. Up narrow wooden stairs and into an attic room which had walls of varnished pine, and a small dormer window which looked out on to the mountains and the valley. There was a double bed but no mattress.

'Miguel has gone back down,' Michael Graves said. 'He says he has to get the things now. It'll take him a few hours.'

'I hope he's going to bring a mattress and intends to get some food. We should have got food down below.'

'There's another floor beneath the kitchen where animals and wood can be kept,' he said.

They walked back down to the ground floor and into the front room. They took chairs out on to the balcony. Katherine lit a cigarette.

'What are you going to do?' Michael Graves asked.

'I'm going to stay,' she said.

'Are you in love with Miguel?'

'I love him, yes.'

'But you're not sure?'

'Of course I'm not sure,' she said.

'Why are you doing this?'

'I'm trusting my luck. I have made up my mind I'm going to stay.'

'You did that today, didn't you?'

'I don't know when I did it. Give me a few minutes – to be quiet.'

They sat in silence as the housemartins swarmed about the village. They listened to the water flowing fast down from the hills above. After a while she spoke again.

'I always feel you live a double life in Barcelona. I think we're just a small part of what you do there.'

'Are you jealous? Do you want me all to yourself?' Michael asked her.

'No, I'm curious. I don't know anything about you.'

'And how eager you are to learn things!'

'Can't we talk directly without you twisting the conversation?'

'You want me to answer your questions?'

'Yes. What sort of teaching will you do in Barcelona?'

'To be straight, I have a job in a school from September teaching English, the language of my forefathers, to adults.'

'So you're going to stay in Spain?'

'I don't know.'

'You'll be able to come and visit us.'

'I've enjoyed meeting you. I like you,' he said, and then he grinned. 'In fact, I almost love you.'

'Every time you start to be serious you make a joke,' she said.

'You grasp things quickly, don't you? You grasped the differences between us more quickly than I did.'

'That wasn't hard, was it?'

'I think you thought that I was the one who burned your house down. I think you thought I'd come back to burn it again. The peasants are revolting,' he laughed.

'How did you know about our house, and how can you make jokes about it?'

'What else can we do? Sing laments?'

'Think about it, perhaps.'

'Or stop thinking about it,' he said and went to the window.

'So is it a joke then in your little town, the Deacons whose house we burned to the ground one night when they were defenceless . . .'

'Hardly defenceless.'

'I was defenceless.'

'I am so glad to be away from it,' he said. 'I am so glad to be away from it.'

*

The sun went blood-red over the mountains in the far distance. Michael Graves lit a fire in the kitchen with some kindling that lay about. Katherine sat on the balcony looking down on the valley feeling the cold encroaching as the night came down. And as the hours went by, as they grew anxious waiting for Miguel, hunger and tiredness made them irritable and silent. They sat in the darkness of the kitchen with the firelight casting bleak shadows on the walls.

*

Several hours passed before the jeep pulled up outside the door. Michael Graves had fallen asleep in the corner, but Katherine had no urge to sleep. She no longer felt even hungry. She woke Michael when she heard the noise of the engine. The driver of the jeep had returned, without Miguel.

Where was he? Katherine asked. The driver was not inclined to answer, but she persisted and he told her that there were problems with the police. However it was not important and would be sorted out in the morning. She asked him where exactly Miguel was and he said in the police station, in Llavorsi – there had been problems.

'*Que pasa con la policía?*' Michael Graves asked. The man was already unloading boxes from the back of the jeep. He repeated that Miguel would be back up in the morning.

Katherine carried a box of candles into the house. There were sheets and blankets in other boxes, as well as food, and mattresses in the back of the jeep. They could not persuade the driver to say anything more about why Miguel was being held in the police station in Llavorsi. When he left they lit candles and sorted out the bed-clothes. She took a candle upstairs to the attic room and Michael helped her carry a mattress up to the bed. He made his own bed in the room beside the kitchen. All night the sound of water rushing from the small hills above them down into the valley kept her awake; all night until just before dawn when the birdsong started and she knew she would have no sleep at all. She went down to the bathroom and washed in cold water. Michael Graves was fast asleep when she glanced into his room.

The sun had not yet risen; there was still a grey shadow over the world below. She walked along a track away from the village; the grass at the side was drenched with dew. As she walked, it grew lighter and she noticed more and more how the colour of the stone in the houses matched the colour of the rock almost exactly. Even the slates on each roof found a match in some shade of the stone behind. The houses could have been caves, so closely were they related to the surrounding rock.

Miguel did not come back that day. The driver brought them enough food to keep hunger at bay: a huge round of rubbery white bread, oil and tomatoes, lettuce, some tins of tuna fish. Michael Graves found more wood for the fire and as evening fell they lit candles. Michael had brought some books which he put on a shelf in the kitchen.

She tried to read but found the flickering of the candle irritating; after a few pages she put the book aside and went to the door. There were lights in a house below, and the sound that Michael Graves had noticed too, of mountain streams in the distance.

In the morning she heard footsteps in the hall downstairs. She had slept soundly and dreamlessly during the night and yet when she heard him in the hall, it was as though she had thought of nothing else since she had seen him last, as though everything had been suspended between the time he left and the time he came back.

She stood in her nightdress at the bottom of the stairs and looked at him. She didn't say anything. He seemed tired and was carrying a few days' growth of beard. Michael Graves came out of the front room wearing only his trousers and immediately began to roar at him and they both started a mock fight with their fists raised, laughing. She rested her shoulder against the wall. She wished Michael Graves would leave them alone.

They did not make love when they went to bed but lay together holding each other.

She lay with her back to him while he explained what had happened. He spoke to her slowly and seemed to choose each word carefully so that she would understand.

Four of them, including Miguel, had stayed in this house in the months after the civil war, he said. Carlos Puig was their leader – Carlos was still in prison in Burgos, although there were rumours now they were going to let him out. Did she understand? That was more than ten years ago. He himself was an anarchist in the province of Lerida. He had burnt the church and the police station in almost every town in Lerida.

Miguel asked her if she understood what he was telling her and she said she did. He had been with Carlos Puig. He wanted her, Katherine, to know they had killed people, including women and children, during the war. And later, when the divisions between them and the other political groups in the war became too great, four of them came here to Pallosa and they attacked from here; they knew how to make bombs and they used them against the police.

He wanted her to know everything – did she understand that he wanted her to know everything? Yes, she told him, she did. They had bombed a policeman's house and they had burnt his wife and children to death. He stopped for a moment and held her. This was more than ten years ago and there was a war on, she must remember that, he whispered. He sighed then, and told her that once they had shot a child who had tried to leave the house. He put his arms around her; there was sweat on his hands.

The war was well over when the police arrested them, he said. He was in Barcelona and they were not sure whether he had been involved with Carlos Puig. They caught the others in the house here in the village with the bombs and everything else. They beat them so badly that one of them, Robert Samaranch, died.

He stopped talking and when he resumed he was almost in tears. He was caught in Barcelona and held for two years, he said; most of the time he was in solitary confinement. Did she understand what that meant? She said she did. The police in Llavorsi now wanted to know why he had come back to the mountains and to this house. They knew who he was. They told him that. But he didn't think there would be any more trouble. Did she understand that? Was it all right?

When he got out of bed to go downstairs she noticed bruises and cuts on his back. She called him then and asked him what had happened. He returned and lay down again, and told her that they had hit him, but not much.

His story stayed with her for days, as though she had eaten something strange and strong, but vaguely familiar.

She kept away from both him and Michael Graves, went walking on her own, went to bed early, sat apart from them on the small balcony in Michael Graves's room smoking and looking out towards the high mountains to the north. An image came to her constantly of a child running for help, running for her life, being run through with bullets, while the thunderous sound of a fire roared in the background.

A Letter from Pallosa

Pallosa
Lerida
Spain
30.5.1952

Dear Mother,

I received your telegram. It frightened me to death when it came. I sat at the table with it in my hand. I was hardly able to open it. I am sorry for not writing and I am sorry, too, that there is not enough news in my letters. I am sorry that you don't know enough about me and I know that you're paying for this and, yes, the money is coming in on time and I am grateful. Does that help?

I will try to write to you. The days go by; there are things to do and things to consider. It is hard, maybe you will understand this, it is hard to do something new now that everything has become habit.

I have thrown in my lot with a man called Miguel whom I met in Barcelona. It is difficult to write about him. There is a solidity about him. I don't know if you know what I mean. He is self-contained. He has been out all day cutting wood; wood, as you can imagine, is important.

But that is not why he is out cutting wood today. Certain things preoccupy him. Our private life, waking to find him wrapped around me, that is what is most real to us. I don't know if you have experienced that. During the day sometimes he hardly notices me. We find things to do. I do not know how long this will last. Maybe you understand why I haven't written about this before. It is not the sort of thing which we talk about normally, is it?

If he ever finds someone who lived here in the past, before the war, the Spanish civil war, he becomes tense. He will seek them out, try and get them on their own, and go over the same things again and again. The same words. I know them now. How there were crops grown here before the war; how there was a mill in Tirvia; which families were fascist and with Franco during the war; what they did in the village after the war.

I am bored by his obsession with the war. I leave him alone when the war comes up. He has found a wood-cutter to talk about life before the war, during the war, after the war and he's even paying him to talk. There will be no wood cut. I know there will be no wood cut.

Our neighbours are not the sort of people you could borrow wood from if you ran out of wood in the winter. Most of the houses in the village are empty and have been since the civil war. Ghosts live in them; old family photos go yellow on the walls; bits and pieces of broken crockery and delft lie broken or chipped in presses. But they are still intact, the twenty or so empty houses, and

I have only been in one or two of them. Some day, a long time from now, they will all fall down and no one will care because no one will ever come back here. The people from here live in Barcelona now, or Lerida, or Gerona.

Three of the houses are occupied, candles burn in them at night. There is Fuster and his wife, quiet and watchful both of them, but intelligent and kind when you need them to be kind. They have children in Barcelona, they have a telephone. We go there sometimes at night and talk to them.

There is no talking to the other two. There is Lidia, who owns the cows, constantly on the look-out for some infringement of her rights which has occurred in the past or is about to occur in the future, constantly urging us to tell her where we married and when. She waters the milk she sells us and some day I will water the money we pay her as well.

I cannot pass her without a conversation. She waylays me, even when I think she is far away and I can escape for a stroll down the village without an interrogation into my past, my present and my future, with constant references to the Virgin Mary, and various other members of the heavenly household, dear to the hearts of Spanish RCs, even when I've watched her moving away, I suddenly find that she has returned to haunt me.

Where did I buy my clothes? Where exactly is Ireland? When am I going to Barcelona next? Why do I have no children? Days go by when I pretend not to know what she's saying.

Her old mother is half her size, permanently encased

in black robes. She squawks at me like an old turkey when I meet her. She speaks only Catalan. Luckily, I don't know a word of it, but I am starting to learn, so soon I may be able to relay to you the wit and wisdom of Lidia's mother. I cannot imagine what it would be like to have lived all your life up here.

There is also a brother, who is a bit soft and visits us every evening before dinner. He met a woman once, Mayte or something was her name, and he was going to marry her. He tells us this each evening. He is funny. He does no work. Lidia does everything. When she gets old she will have nobody and this place will be even more forsaken than it is now. Her brother will be no use to her anyway. I have fantasies of her starving to death some winter. I mustn't be too hard on her. It is not easy.

We don't speak to the other family at all. I think Miguel has been rude to them. They are the Matarós. Their house is the biggest house and they own a jeep. There is a family with one daughter aged about twenty-five and an older woman who is a sister of either the husband or wife. A few months went by in the winter when we didn't see the sister at all and I have a feeling that there are others inside the house whom we haven't seen yet, just like in *Jane Eyre*, and Miguel thinks I am probably right. We wait patiently for some of them to appear and I will let you know as soon as this happens.

There is something else that has been on my mind and I will say it to you now. We were burned out during the Troubles in Ireland. You and I have never talked of this, which is odd, as we have spoken frankly about other things. We were burned out during the Troubles. I put it bluntly down now and I hope that you're still reading. This is how I put it. But it isn't exactly what happened, is it?

We weren't burned out, because we didn't leave, we built a new house which still stands and we built it fast. But you were burned out because you left then and you've never been back; no matter what my father said about how safe we were, you stayed in London. I am your only child. I saw you for holidays and we never talked about what happened that night in all the years.

The locals turned on us. That's what happened. That's what the Troubles were for us. The time the locals turned on us. That's what happened in Ireland in 1920. I don't remember a fire, but I remember a sound, like a big wind, and being carried. I don't remember seeing the fire, I must have been three years old. I remember staying in Bennett's Hotel in Enniscorthy. I'll never forget the sound of the wind. What do you remember? Please tell me what happened. How did you get out? How did I get out? How many of them came? Why did you leave and never come back?

I always believed that what happened to us was an act of evil, something vicious done, that when tension was high it was us they would go after – they would round on us, the locals. No good came of it. Did it? I want to know about it, so I can think about it. It has become important. If you want me to write to you, I'm afraid you'll have to take me seriously. It's not easy to write like this.

Yours with love as always,
    Katherine

The Magic Mountain

Calm, quiet days in the Pyrenees. The sharp chill of winter yielding to the subtle movements of spring. The foresters were at work in the hills above the village. She watched the elaborate ritual of felling a tree, the long preparations, the shouting, the resting periods. She was intrigued by the unsettling of nature at its source, the disturbed insect life, bird life, wildlife. And what was left behind resembled a battle scene: stumps of trees, blocks of wood, loose briars, brambles, a shorn world still wrapped in by the forest, an oasis of hurt.

She followed the foresters with oil and board and a small easel and she painted the felling of trees, the havoc. She was fascinated by the new colours of dead wood, of wounded stumps by the small clearing in the forest breathing in freely while it could.

The foresters started at dawn. She got up and left Miguel sleeping, his warm body in the bed. It was always freezing and it was too cold to wash. She put her clothes on as quickly as she could, layer after layer of vests and pullovers. She made a flask of coffee, put bread and cheese into a bag which she carried on her back as she did the easel and canvas. Covering herself with a huge rug, she set off in the early morning to the place where the foresters were working a mile or two away. She wore a woollen scarf on her head.

The foresters were already at work clearing the pine trees from the skirting of a small side road. She could place herself far back and paint the devastation they had caused. She mixed colours carefully: the oily brown, fresh green, withered yellow mingling with the flat, cold blue of the sky, the remnants of frost and snow and the beginnings of spring when the world starts to open up.

She had seen an exhibition in London of paintings from the First World War, pictures of landscape as wreck, as a place where men died brutally and cruelly. She had in mind a number of pictures, she could not remember by whom, in which nature itself was the subject, the battlefield as a mutation, as a perversity, in which the violence was done to the natural order, to animals, to birds and insects, to fields and flowers. It was just such a sense of the world and its order and disorder that she wanted for these paintings.

Music came to her all morning as she worked, snatches of tunes listened to the night before, whole arias, or just the feeling in a piece that she had listened to. Michael Graves had brought them the music. He came and went: sometimes they had no idea where he went, but mostly he went back to Barcelona and made what money he could teaching and drawing. She missed him; she had become close to him. Once or twice he had arrived in a state of dejection: ill, broke, quiet, going for walks on his own or staying in bed and not getting up until the evening. But his spirits were usually high, he generally wanted to stay up all night talking. Each time he came he brought them presents.

He came with an old record player he had bought in Barcelona with a handle to wind it up and replacement needles. It worked perfectly. He brought a big box of records and each time thereafter he added to the collection. At first she thought she would never get to hear them all, there were so many. Michael put himself in charge of the record player. He selected everything and introduced every piece of music, sometimes not telling them what it was until it was over. Miguel was familiar with some of the operas and could sing along and recognise tunes; but Michael knew everything, even the Italian or French words. He had heard it all before in Enniscorthy, he said. Katherine had heard nothing before. She didn't believe him about Enniscorthy.

Symphonies, songs, chamber music, opera arias, sacred music, sonatas, concertos. The records consisted mostly of excerpts. Michael told her the story of Madame Butterfly and she listened as he put the needle down and the static came loud and clear followed by the voice: *Un bel di Vedremo*. He played her Claudia Muzio singing the great aria from *Tosca*: 'I have lived for art, I have lived for love.' He sang it himself before he put it on and told her how poor Tosca had done nothing to deserve her fate. He sang it again. *Vissi d'arte, vissi d'amore*. He put the needle down and the magic happened. He played her arias from the great French operas: Gigli singing from *Samson et Dalila*; the tenor and baritone duet from *The Pearl Fishers*; the soldiers' prayer from Gounod's *Faust*.

Long nights in the Pyrenees. Darkness fell at four in

the deep days of winter. They lit candles and stoked up the fire in the kitchen. She tried to learn Catalan from Miguel. She tried to imitate the guttural clipped accent he used when he spoke Catalan. At first she spoke it as a joke, using just the phrases she knew, trying to put nouns and verbs together to form sentences. When she went for the milk every day down in the village she talked to the peasants in Catalan, but had immense difficulty understanding anything they said.

Slowly it became a language they used between themselves, not replacing Spanish which they still spoke when it was vital that what they said was understood. Slowly it became like the record player on the shelf in the kitchen or the fierce cold of winter, slowly it became another pattern in the fabric they had woven for themselves.

Money too became part of the pattern. It left London and her mother's bank account on the first day of every third month to arrive in the bank in Tremp some time afterwards, usually a week, sometimes more and once, to their consternation, it did not arrive for a month. Money came too from Miguel's gallery in Barcelona, but not much. They lived on her mother's money. One month in every three they lived well, buying cheeses and cured meat in bulk, vats of wine, cognac, chocolate, American cigarettes. When this ran out they were back to rice and lentils until the money came again.

Jordi Gil brought them what materials they needed. He always came in a car with a roof rack to take down some paintings to sell in Barcelona. Miguel worked hard before Jordi Gil's visits. He became interested in mirrors and tried to paint a reflected world, scenes turned upside down, or events distorted in a false mirror. Katherine did not like them, but Gil seemed to think they would sell. Gil would only spend a few hours at the house and then make the long journey back to Barcelona. Katherine made him stay for lunch, put good wine on the table and a strong fire in the grate.

Katherine had placed her own work against the walls of the front room, unframed. There were five or six large paintings of the felling of the trees and many smaller ones, including studies and drawings. She did not want Miguel in the room when Jordi Gil looked at her work, she was nervous about it; Miguel had paid little attention to her painting and she didn't want him to witness any comment on it now.

She waited until the lunch was finished that day and Miguel's new paintings had been examined and were being bundled together. She whispered to Jordi Gil that she had something she wanted him to look at, but she didn't want Miguel to know. She made him think that they were paintings by Miguel.

She instructed him to tell Miguel he needed a breath of air, he was going for a short walk. Miguel was down in the long room at the end of the house and did not notice them going into the front room. Jordi Gil looked at the paintings. He picked up one of the smaller ones and examined it carefully. She had not signed it. He closed the door behind them and looked at the bigger ones. He did not speak to her. He kept moving from painting to painting. He said that he liked them, rubbed his head and smiled.

They walked back down to the long room where Miguel was battling with paper and twine. Jordi Gil told him that he had signed up a new artist. Miguel smiled and looked puzzled. Jordi Gil took him down to look at Katherine's paintings. She waited in the kitchen.

He took the work to Barcelona and Michael Graves saw some of it hanging in the gallery and wrote to her. Some of it was sold. Michael Graves found a poster and print shop that had just opened in Barcelona; he told her the prices were high but advised her to use the gallery money to buy reproductions. She told Jordi Gil to allow Michael Graves a certain amount of money. Day after day long cardboard telescope-shaped containers came with the jeep that collected the milk from the village. He sent her van Gogh's *Self Portrait* and his painting of Arles at night; he sent her Rembrandt's painting of an *Old Man* and Titian's painting of *A Young Man With A Glove*; he sent her Picasso's blue paintings. He sent her posters of new exhibitions in Paris – Braque, Kandinsky, Paul Klee – which had been on sale in Barcelona. She plastered the walls with the reproductions.

She felt an urge to acquire things, pieces of furniture, these reproductions, new records. She felt an urge to anchor herself in this house in the mountains.

At night Katherine and Miguel got into the bed like children and tried to fend off the cold by huddling together, holding onto each other for warmth under a huge mound of blankets. After a while desire began to ooze between them, another form of heat, and slowly they would make love in the dark room, with the candle out and the blankets undisturbed. They were ravenous for each other.

She asked Miguel if he was happy and he said that he was. He told her he dreamed of being able to live here after the war. He never imagined that they would lose the war. In the early days of the war, they took over a print shop in Lerida and he made posters there, everyone knew things would change, he said, but no one believed they would end. Finally, he told her, they were betrayed by everybody, not just by the fascists, but by the Catalan nationalists and the communists. He fought the war for her again and what had happened became clearer. It seemed so far away from them now: the excitement, the new world that he believed in and wanted to make. The words he used were difficult for her: she did not understand fully when he talked about *freedom, anarchy, revolution.* He had experienced something that she could only imagine. Once or twice, she felt that she would like to have known him then.

She never knew the mountains as he did. He could always find a pathway that she had not noticed. He walked for miles every day with no purpose in mind. Once or twice he showed her where he had hidden after the war, small cabins and ruined houses.

He came back one day earlier than usual; he surprised her in the kitchen where she was washing potatoes. He brought her down to the big window in the long room to look out. It was the first snow; they would be snowed in for a month at least, the snow would lie on the ground for three months. He held her around the waist as she looked out. The memory of this day became as fixed as the rock all around: the memory of watching the first snow and the expectation of being there together, closed in, immune, ready for any happiness that came their way.

Dublin: 1955

The Royal Hibernian Hotel, Dawson Street, Dublin. The early morning. From the window she could see Leinster House, where the new Parliament sat, from where Ireland regulated its own affairs. From the window too she could see the grey sky hanging over Dublin, promising rain. For two weeks the sky had been like this, darkening slowly in the late morning or the early afternoon. In the hours between three and five the rain came; for over a week now she had spent the day listlessly watching it, watching the rain pelt down on Molesworth Street.

Whenever it brightened she went out and walked up to Saint Stephen's Green; sometimes the grey clouds parted to allow glimpses of a summer evening. Each time she moved from the hotel she searched faces in the street at random for a hint of recognition; for one instant she was absolutely sure she must know each face she encountered, and was almost ready to cry out, to say something. It did not feel like a foreign country, but a world she had known at some time in the past, but could not now reconstruct fully or recollect completely: a world peopled by relatives, ancestors, friends, peopled by faces she was just one step from being able to name or associate with some event.

The buildings on Grafton Street were much lower than she had remembered. But the faces, each face as it came towards her, struck a chord. She stared at people and they stared back. She was desperate.

The letter to Tom lay on the mantelpiece in the room. She had sealed the envelope and was grateful that she could not re-read the letter she had written him almost ten days before. But it was brief and to the point. *I am in Dublin. I want to see you about certain matters and will wait here until I do so. Kindly contact me.* She picked up the phone and rang down to reception.

'Could I please have my breakfast up here? Yes, and there's a letter I want posted – could you arrange that for me? It's rather urgent. Thank you.' She went back to the window and stood watching the grey morning. The letter lay on the mantelpiece; she could tear it up, pay her bill and leave without seeing him. Her courage could fail her and it was simply a matter of courage; in any case, she had no reason to face him other than to extract what she wanted. There was no sentimentality in her calculations, she could do without him.

The maid came with the breakfast tray and left it on the table.

'I called down to say that I had a letter to post,' she said. 'It's there on the mantelpiece. It's very urgent.'

'It'll be sent out immediately,' the woman said.

'Now?' she asked.

'If you like, the porter can take it down to the GPO this instant.'

'Yes, I would be very grateful.'

There was still time to go to the phone to cancel the letter, to tell them not to send it, to decide to wait for a day or two. And when she didn't ring down, when she had finished her breakfast and was fully dressed, she knew she had better be ready for him, that it was only a matter of days now before she would be blamed and accused, and would have no answer or excuse, when there would be no forgiveness.

She regretted now that she had not specified how he should contact her. He could arrive unannounced at the hotel. As the day went by, she tried to imagine what he would do when he got her letter, how he would react. She began to think of him. It was five years since she had left, it would be exactly five in September. He would be fifty-three now, fifteen years older than she, he would not have changed much except that he might be balder, stockier.

She had lunch in her room with wine and a gin afterwards to make her sleep. Her dreams in the afternoon were vivid and close to her; they left their mark on what remained of the day.

She imagined Tom quiet, determined, composed. She saw him opening the letter in the evening when his day's work was done, when he had washed, shaved and changed into a tweed jacket and cavalry twill trousers, after a dinner which he would have eaten mostly in silence.

Richard would be there now, fifteen years old, settling into his father's ways, and there would mostly be silence between them but no strain. Her name would not have been mentioned between them in five years.

Tom would wait for a day or two before responding; he would leave her time. He was careful, cautious, judicious. She didn't want time; she was ready to face him. He would not use the telephone or send a telegram; he cared too much for his privacy and these offered no privacy. He would write; she awaited a letter. Hers had been posted on Monday and his reply arrived on Friday. It was short and curt as her own had been. *Will see you at hotel, Monday 5 pm.* That was all.

She saw him as soon as he came into the lounge. His hair was greyer than before, but that was the only change. She had bought new clothes in the morning and had been to a hairdresser which had helped her feel ready for him. She stood up.

'How long have you been in Dublin?' he asked immediately.

'I've been here for two weeks. How are you?' She held out her hand.

'I thought the date on your letter was a mistake.' He held her hand for a moment, then let go.

'Yes, I didn't send it for a while after I wrote it.'

'Do sit down,' he said. She sat with her back to the wall, he sat opposite her.

'I had business to do, so it was easy for me to come,' he said.

'I hoped you would have come anyway.' She smiled.

'Your mother wrote to tell me you are living in a house in the mountains without water and electricity. Is that true?'

'My mother interferes.'

'I want to know how you are living.'

'Did my mother not put all that in her letter?'

'Her letter was almost as brief as yours. She wrote that you had been living in the mountains without water or electricity and she wished me to know that you had her backing in anything you now wanted to do. She made it sound as though there was something specific you wanted to do.'

'There is.'

'What is it?' he asked.

'I'll tell you in a moment. I want a drink and I want to know about Richard.' Tom went to the bar and she wrapped her arms around herself as though some awful cold had come down into the wide, rich room of the hotel.

'I didn't plan to tell you this,' she said when Tom came back, 'but I dream all the time about you and Richard and the house. I dream that I go back there, I appear in the kitchen just as you are sitting down to eat. Richard can see me but you can't. His eyes follow me, but he doesn't move or say anything. I want to touch him and talk to him and hold him in my arms. But all he does is watch me. And when I wake up I feel empty and forlorn. I know that I have ruined things. I know that. I'm sorry. Tom, I'm sorry.'

'This is very difficult,' he said, 'it's very difficult to talk here.'

'Do you want to move?'

'Where to? I can't think of anywhere.'

'Tell me about Richard,' she said.

'He's been at Saint Columba's now for three years. He's only got two years more.'

'What will he do then?'

'There's always plenty to do at home but he's been in Scotland staying with his cousins every summer now and I think he'll go to a college there for a few years.'

'What sort of college?' She tried to picture Scotland and the dreary cousins.

'Oh, where he'll learn about agriculture and farming so that when he takes over he'll know what to do. He knows the farm pretty well.'

'Tom, I want to sell my part of the farm. That's what I'm here for.'

'It doesn't belong to you,' he said quickly, 'you can't sell it.' He seemed instantly angry.

'It was mine before we married, it's mine now. I want to sell it, Tom.' She could feel the blood reddening her face.

'I wouldn't have come to meet you if I'd known you were going to want something like this.'

'I need the money. I have a different life now and I want to sell. You have your own farm. I'm going to sell whether you like it or not.'

'You have no rights. The farm belongs to me, both farms belong to me, and Richard will get both of them. You will sell nothing.'

'It's my farm.'

'Go to a solicitor then and find out. You have no right to sell, the property is mine, go and check it. I don't mind what embarrassment you cause me. I have sat so many nights thinking about you.' His voice had quietened. She had never heard him talk like this before – she found it difficult to believe him.

'I have thought of you too,' she said.

'Think of me now, then, and think about Richard. I want you to come back with me. I have told Richard I'm meeting you. I have told him that I will ask you to come back.'

'You shouldn't have done that.'

'I did it because I meant it. Seriously, I want you to come back now.'

'Tom, listen to me. I married you and when I did I owned a large house and three hundred acres. It was in my mother's name then, but it was mine. Are you telling me that I own nothing now and you will let me have nothing?' She tried to change her tone, to speak more quietly and firmly.

'What's ours is Richard's, it's for him, it's not for us to sell, no matter how badly we behave.'

'Will you buy it from me?'

'I don't need to buy it from you. I own it, but it's not mine to sell or buy or dispose of. I told Richard I would ask you to come back. Do you wish me to tell him you want to sell half his land?'

'You will tell him what you like. You can tell him his mother is impoverished.'

'I can't talk to you here.'

She did not answer immediately, she didn't know what he wanted: did he want to leave the hotel and walk the streets with her, did he want to move to her room, or did he just want to talk somewhere more private?

'Do you want to come upstairs?' she said.

'Where?'

'To my room.'

'All right,' he said, and stood up hesitantly. She had the key with her and she beckoned him to follow her towards the staircase.

★

Once in the room she closed the door and leaned against it looking at him. It was now clear that he had aged more than five years. As he went to the window and looked out, she noticed that he had developed a slight stoop and his face had thickened. She could hear herself breathing.

'I've never been upstairs in this hotel before,' he said. 'What made you choose it?'

She didn't reply. He stayed at the window looking out. 'It's frightful weather,' he said. 'It's been a dreadful summer.' She went over and stood beside him at the window and looked out too.

'Yes,' she said, 'it's been very dull here.'

She turned around and put her head on his shoulder – at first he did not respond, but stayed there dead still as though he was embarrassed, his hands hanging by his sides. After a while he held her and moved her towards the bed where he lay beside her. He took his jacket off and his shoes. For a long time he held her against him, saying nothing. Until the light outside began to fade they lay there, together.

'Tom,' she said, 'put your hands on my tummy.'

'Why?' he asked.

'You won't be able to feel it yet because it's too small, but soon you will. I'm pregnant. I'm going to have a baby in the New Year.'

'I don't want to put my hands down,' he said. His voice was low.

'I'm going back,' she whispered. 'I'm going to have a child.'

He rolled away from her and sat on the side of the bed.

'You're pregnant. Are you sure?'

'Yes.'

'Who's the father? Can I ask?'

'Don't ask.'

'I'm going to go now,' he said quietly. 'I would like to have an address for you.'

'My mother always knows where I am.'

'Will you be here for long?' She could hear him putting on his shoes.

'No, I will go as soon as I can.'

'Could you wait for a few days? I will send you a cheque. Can you wait?' His voice was subdued.

'Yes, I can.'

'Wait then. I must go now.' He put his two hands on her arm and held her for a moment before he left the room.

Isona

Even months later the memory of the pain stayed with her, the shock of the pain. She had bought a jeep so that when the time came, there would be a way of getting her down the mountain to help, if help was needed. She tried to teach Miguel to drive but he was impatient and useless behind the wheel. She would have to let someone in the village drive down.

The first pain she felt was like a period pain, but when it came again she knew what it was. She could not make it to the unused stone church to ring the bells as she had arranged to do; she called from the window but there was no response. When the first contractions came she had to lie down. She had no idea how the child would be delivered. It seemed too big, it seemed impossible. They sent for the midwife. When Miguel came Katherine told him the baby was going to die. For hours and hours she believed this and she told it to anyone who came into the room.

She wanted it to die, to lie still and die. It was the life in it which tore her. All night Miguel held her hand and she whispered to him that she wanted the child to die.

The night would not end. When she asked what time

it was they told her it was three in the morning. She asked the midwife what time the child would come, and the midwife said it was difficult, it could take a long time.

'Am I going to die?' she said in English. It had not occurred to her before, but when she looked at the midwife's face, it struck her, it struck her that she was going to die and the child was going to live.

'Miguel, Miguel!' she shouted as loudly as she could; he came bounding up the wooden stairs.

'*Qué pasa? Qué pasa?*'

'*Me voy a morir? Me voy a morir?*'

'No.'

'*Seguro? Estás seguro?*'

He did not move from the bed again. His denial that she would die did not reassure her; he had accepted her question as natural, had been too quick to answer it. The midwife wanted her to relax, but Katherine watched her eyes for some sign. The pain came back with the contractions. The baby would live, she knew, but the baby would kill her. And they would bury her as soon as they could, and the child would live. The child was too big not to kill her.

In the last few months as the baby grew bigger, she and Miguel had spent most of the time in bed together, wrapped up against the cold. In the few hours of daylight she covered herself up and went down to the workroom to draw and paint. She drew the room with a pencil and coloured in only what could be seen through the window, the wide white air, the mountains in the distance, odd rough stone buildings. She gave the room a spare domesticity by moving only a table against the wall and putting a few jugs on it and a chair beside it at an angle as though someone had just been sitting there. She made the room seem dark, sketchy and unfinished. She had done one or two of these a day on small sheets of white paper. That's what would be left now, these small things drawn when she was happy, when there was energy to spare. Some people would know that they had been done in the months before she died.

She hardly remembered giving birth. She remembered very little once the midwife cut her with what she thought was scissors. She remembered that she cried. She remembered that Miguel held her hand and told her she was well.

Months later the scars and bitterness remained. She had not wanted a child; she was not prepared to go through such fear and agony. It had been easier when Richard was born, the midwife could not believe that this was her second child. And then they had presented the child to her, clean, swaddled, quiet. It was a girl, they told her as they put new sheets on her bed and took the other ones away, *una noia*. She had not wanted to be diverted thus into caring for a child, feeding the child, nursing it. She had not sought any of this. She could not tell anyone how much she believed the whole thing had diminished her.

She took the baby into her arms; she was tiny, a small shadow of black hair on her head. As the months went by she watched, amazed by the baby's absolute trust, by the calm way the baby looked at her. It had not been like this when Richard was a baby. The baby smiled more when Miguel was there to play with her and make sounds and faces to amuse her.

Summer came around again. In front of the house the baby lay in a pram. Miguel wanted to call her Isona. They sat in easy chairs drinking wine in the afternoon. The hot sun shone down on the Pyrenees. Soon they would need to start getting wood in again for the winter.

A Diary: 1957

Pallosa, 23 June 1957

This morning when I woke up I could hear Isona in the room downstairs. She was standing leaning against the bars of the cot, crying, and as soon as I came in she began to laugh. Her face lit up. She put her arms out to me and I picked her up. She was all wet. She kept laughing as I carried her into the kitchen. Sometimes it is wonderful having her here to trust me and to love me the way she does.

There is no one here who will understand how much at certain times she looks like my father, how a look comes on her face and she becomes the image of him. Richard had that too when he was her age, although they don't look alike in any other way. We have removed her from a world where that sort of recognition means anything. We are her only roots, no one comes before us.

She will never know where she came from, where we came from, the accidents that have brought her into the world. I would love her to know the house I come from, the river, the farm. I would love it if we could all meet sometime, Richard, Tom, Miguel, Isona, Michael Graves. I would love to see Richard picking her up and carrying her. I'm afraid I have placed myself beyond all that.

Things are difficult with Miguel now. I had a nightmare. I woke in the night, still screaming, I couldn't stop the dream, even though I was wide awake and Miguel was holding me, it stayed on and I was afraid to sleep it was so real and close, I believed it would start happening again.

I dreamed about the fire. I dreamed about being led down through the long corridors of the big old house, a man behind me, guiding me along, with all the rooms on fire and the corridor running on and on until we came to the stairs. I could feel his hand on my neck guiding me. The dream was as real to me as being here now in the kitchen after dinner and the pen in my hand.

When we got to the door we couldn't get out, there were men waiting outside for us and one of the men was Miguel. They had guns. He had a gun and he was shooting at me. I feel afraid again as I write this down, it was so bad. It was ghastly. I don't know who it was behind me but when I woke up I thought it was Tom. I woke up when the bottom of my nightdress caught fire. I couldn't believe the fire had stopped, even though Miguel kept telling me that I was fine, that there was nothing to worry about.

I told him about the dream. I told him things I had not told him before. I told him about the men setting fire to the house in Enniscorthy and about us running out in our bare feet in the middle of the night. I had not told him any of this before. He understood. He asked me questions about Ireland and about Irish politics, but I only knew that this had happened to us and to others like us before the British left.

He was puzzled by this new context he had for me, as though I was some sort of victim of history. Not a victim, perhaps, but a participant. I have failed to explain to him that I am not. I am on my own here without all that weight of history and I differ from him in the way I manage. He's decided I am someone who was on the wrong side of a war. I am sorry I told him anything. I am as innocent as our child.

Miguel has gone down to Fuster's house. He took down the beer I brought up from Llavorsi today. They will talk about the war, what happened before the war, the war they had. When I have washed up I will go down and join them, have a few drinks. I hope Isona sleeps all night. I hope things get better between us.

A Letter to Michael Graves

Pallosa

1 May 1958

Dear Michael Graves,

Miguel, you will be glad to know, has discovered illness and is thoroughly enjoying himself wrapped up in bed with a walking stick to hand so he can bang on the floor when he wants something. He says he is not growing a beard but he refuses all offers of a razor, soap and a mirror. I'm not sure I want him to have a beard.

He has become addicted to soup, which he says is much easier to eat than meat and vegetables when you're in bed. He's been lying up there for ten days now. Sometimes he coughs just to let me know that he's still suffering from a bad cold, or flu, but most of the time he sits up with a sketch pad resting on his knees drawing very unlikely faces. He says he may never get up again, but he has to move at least once a day, as I refuse to come up and down the stairs with a chamber pot, despite his requests that I do so. I have told him that I may go to bed myself soon too, as I'm not in the full bloom of health either and he says I will be very welcome but we'll have to put Isona into an orphanage.

Isona, who has now fallen asleep, has been a nuisance all morning. Her cheeks are red from moaning and crying. I try to send her up to her father but Miguel has developed a cunning way of forcing her to come back down again. I think he just ignores her. Yesterday she came down crying and said he was making faces at her. She won't stop crying and whingeing. I began to cry as well when she cried at me. She hates that and I have made myself stop. There's no point in making the child more of a monster than she already is.

Miguel has good reason to stay in bed. What will happen when he gets up again is beyond me. He has been involved in a running battle with Mataró. The reason for this battle is as clear to you as it is to me. Miguel doesn't like Mataró because he is a fascist. I don't know if he is a fascist. Do you know anything about that? Anyway, Miguel has been making every effort to have a fight with him since the day we arrived here. The only reason such a battle has been avoided is that Mataró is too stupid to understand the sort of thing that Miguel has been shouting at him, or too deaf. I think actually he is a bit deaf.

The women in Mataró's life are much put upon, as you know. His wife and daughter run if they see me coming. They're like a pair of idiot nuns. Why the daughter, whatever her name is, is dressed in black, I have never understood. They look like small fierce birds, both of them, and they oppress me whenever I think of them. I don't often think of them. Someone wanted to send for them when I was in the middle of giving birth to Isona, and one of the things that made Miguel laugh most was the idea of the two of them arriving up in the bedroom with me squealing like a pig on the bed. They give me the creeps.

Maria Mataró, the sister, did attend the birth – as you know, I think she is treated like dirt over there. Mrs Fuster says they don't feed her. I think there's a screw loose. I think she needs treatment. Her head rocks around on her shoulders when she walks, as if there was a whole set of crucial muscles missing. She watches our house like a hawk. If there's any sign of our going out, down to Tirvia, or just out for a walk, we will always look over and find that she has stepped out on the balcony and is glaring over at us.

We have tried to lock the house a number of times. It is so easy to enter from the stables below here, despite Miguel's barriers. Maria Mataró seems to have no problem getting in. Miguel says she gets under the door like a rat and this indeed may be true. She takes food. She has a particular fondness for high-protein food. Cheese – if there is cheese she will devour it – and red meat or even chicken.

She doesn't seem to take food out of the house, preferring, it appears, to consume it within our walls – which makes her chances of being caught much higher. She likes milk as well. Having stuffed herself – and she will eat any amount of cheese – she will go upstairs and root in the presses and the wardrobe. She steals stockings and my underwear. She seems to try things on and if she doesn't like them she will cast them aside. She never cleans up after herself.

Miguel has tried every method of provoking a row

with Mataró. In fact, if I remember well, you and he created a disturbance outside the Mataró headquarters, probably driving his wife and poor daughter into a further state of disarray, on one of your rare visits to these parts. No doubt, now that I have reminded you, you will recall that you roared abuse of a very personal nature about Mataró all night. This is the sort of campaign Miguel has been conducting over the years. Fuster, who is the only sane man in the village, dislikes all of this and I have to listen to him rabbiting on about how Mataró is in with the police. Sometimes I dread meeting him when I know Miguel has been abusive. Then Miguel quietens down for a while. Maybe the moon starts to wane – don't know why – and I have peace. Then it starts again. Miguel starts to separate Mataró's sheep from the flock. I don't know what else he does. In the meantime, according to Fuster, Mataró is buying up every bit of land he can get his hands on.

I asked Miguel to forget about him, to keep his mind on us, to get on with his work. I said various things to Miguel. His mind is not like mine; he is stubborn and obtuse, he fixes on things. Sometimes this is very funny, for a whole long night he can pretend we are in Mataró's house, he is Mataró and the three women, and I am a visitor. You know how he can keep this going, and I will encourage him, you know that too. But in the end it makes me feel forlorn, this time misspent.

You couldn't like Mataró. His bad manners and his mean scowl may have been exaggerated by Miguel, but he does seem unpleasant. His wife and daughter I could also do without and I hate his sister smelling around my bedroom. But they were here first, they own property here. They have a right to be left alone, as long as she stops stealing.

It is unlikely now that she will steal again. We went out for a walk, it must have been three weeks ago, and we saw her watching us from the balcony of Mataró's house. The hunger must have been eating away at her, poor thing, but we had hidden every single comestible in the house. Miguel said he wanted to go back and I carried on for a while with Isona and we went as far as the stream so she could sail her boat.

When I returned to the house I could hear the screaming and shouting. Miguel had caught Maria, and it only struck me then that he had gone back especially to catch her. He had dragged her back over to Mataró's house and all the noise was coming from there. He had the key to the door so I waited for him on the steps of the house. Odd shouts still rose from Mataró's house as time went by. His face was pale when he came back. Mataró will be feeding his own sister in future, he said, or something like that.

Later, when it was dark, he went out again. I thought he was going to Fuster's house, as he often does. I think I was trying to sew, or wash, or do something unpleasant in the kitchen. When he came back he had a chair, a good strong kitchen chair, which he put in front of me. 'Do you know where I got that from?' he said. 'No,' I replied. 'I stole it from Mataró's house,' he said.

This is the chair I am sitting on as I write this letter. The other one, which he stole just before he fell ill, is upstairs beside the bed. I rest the tray with the soup on it. Mataró stopped me the other day – in all the years in this village he has never addressed me before or even nodded at me – and asked me if I had seen two chairs which had gone missing from his house. I didn't reply. He said maybe Lidia had them. I said maybe his sister had them; had he spoken to her? He muttered to himself and walked past me. Maybe in ten years' time he will speak to me again.

I have told you before that the police in Llavorsi have taken to stopping me to check my driving licence and delay me generally whenever I go down in the jeep. I hope they don't come looking for the chairs.

I am writing this late at night. Miguel is asleep and has pulled all the blankets over to his side of the bed. I am tired and soon I will have to go upstairs and wake him up to equalise the distribution of our blankets. This is married life, from which you have protected yourself. I have spent three hours pacifying Isona. Every time I moved she cried. When I gave her her food she cried, when I read her a story she cried – she wanted another story, a different one – when I tried to get her to sit on her potty she cried.

Then she discovered that it was time to go to bed. She actually hit me on the face in temper. She kicked me. I don't know what I'm going to do with her. It's just a phase, Fuster's wife tells me it's just a phase. There was a time when she was a little angel, when she would smile at me at night before she went to sleep. At the end of next summer I will take her down to school in Tirvia every morning and she will have another set of people to think about and kick when she feels bad. Still, she exhausts me. She takes up most of the day.

If her father weren't so funny and so handsome, he would be a burden with his obsessions, his irrational feeling that he owns this village or has some special rights here, which are not shared by Mataró. At night sometimes, we drink hot wine before we go to bed and he will talk again about what happened after the civil war. I know he has talked to you about this too. I have asked you before if you think he is making any of it up. I know that you told me it was an unfair question. I know it was deeply disloyal. I also know that you believe him. I believe him.

I am putting this in writing now, here, late at night when they are asleep. This war has not ended yet, in his eyes, or in anybody else's. Do you remember our first night in this room, when I said to you that I hoped Miguel's disappearance was the worst thing that would ever happen to us here and you became agitated and told me to stop talking like that? It was as though you had seen something. I have seen something too, not a ghost, or anything unearthly. I have not had visions. I just know that I have taken on more than I can deal with.

The twilights are heartbreakingly beautiful. I wait for them, the sun making a red band against the few clouds that have gathered on the horizon, the thick yellow light. I work when I can. Miguel says he will start working again soon. We'd love you to come and visit us, now that we have new chairs.

Yours with love,
    Katherine

Carlos Puig

In the dead of December that same year Miguel went
down to Barcelona and came back with Carlos Puig.
Katherine recognised the name as soon as he said it.
Miguel had found him in Barcelona, alone, lost,
incapable, broken, after eighteen years in Burgos prison.
Carlos Puig smiled at her, his eyes searching and eager.
He stayed for hours at the window in the room beside
the kitchen, a blanket wrapped around him, looking out
at the mountains.

Sometimes he seemed like an old man, his hair grey
and his teeth yellow, but when he turned to thank her
for food she had brought him, or another blanket, she
could catch a glimpse for a moment of someone else.

Katherine was frightened by the absences in him. She
sat with him sometimes, but never tried to speak. Isona
was learning to talk and Miguel moved the playpen into
the workroom where Carlos Puig slept. For the first few
days the child took no notice of him, talked to herself,
cried, or wanted to be lifted by Katherine or Miguel as
though Carlos Puig was not in the room. One day
Katherine noticed that Isona had let a wooden brick fall
beyond her reach and was calling for it to be handed

back to her. She watched Carlos Puig move and give it to the child. Isona examined the brick carefully and then searched Carlos Puig's face. Again she threw the brick out of the playpen. He leant down and lifted it up and handed it to her. She did it again, laughing this time – she was growing brave. Carlos Puig smiled as he handed it to her.

Isona was two now. When she woke in the morning she would demand to be let down to Carlos's room with her bricks or toys. She talked to him as though he were a child, and sometimes he answered her. She imposed a strain on him that on occasions he could not bear and he would lie on the bed with his face in the pillow and Isona would go to find Katherine.

What was he like before the war? Katherine imagined him as gentle, refined, quiet. Miguel laughed at her. No, he was a journalist, not a rich journalist or even very famous but, Miguel said, he was nasty. When he wrote for the anarchist newspaper his scorn was special. He knew how to hate, that was why Miguel liked him. He was from an ordinary family in Barcelona and spoke Catalan. He used his pen, until words were no good, Miguel looked at her, and then Carlos used bombs, he explained. And when the war was over, and the Republican leaders had gone into exile, he stayed behind and used more bombs.

'*La policía sabe que está aquí?*' she asked. He told her that when the police noticed him, they would come to see what he was doing. There was one man in the police station at Llavorsi who remembered everything: Sust, a Catalan. He knew Miguel, had already questioned him, and knew Carlos Puig. Should we leave, she asked him. Wait, he told her, wait and see!

In the spring Michael Graves came to stay. He put his huge canvas bag on the table and emptied it. Isona watched carefully as he took out a duck that walked when you wound it up. She ran to show it to Carlos. Michael Graves called her back and gave her a mouth organ to give to Carlos as well; they listened in the kitchen to see if he would make a sound with it, but nothing happened. He brought Katherine paint and brushes.

'You look very happy,' he said to her.

'Do I?' she asked. 'Do I?'

They put a bed for Michael Graves in the front room. In a few days Michael Graves had managed to find out a great deal. Michael Graves told them that Carlos still believed that they were going to come after him. He had told Michael Graves that he often saw them around the house. Katherine said there had been no one around the house. Michael Graves repeated what Carlos had said.

She wondered how Michael had found out so much. Her efforts to talk to Carlos Puig had come to nothing and Miguel hardly took any notice of him. As the weather became finer Miguel and Michael Graves went for long walks across the mountains, often disappearing for days at a time. They left Katherine there, as she wanted to be left, to work on drawings and paintings of Isona and Carlos Puig.

Katherine had difficulty understanding what Carlos Puig said, and did not know whether he was whispering to himself or trying to talk to her. That day, he was deeply troubled, she could feel a sense of longing in him, he was trying to say something. He continued to whisper and search her face. His eyes were clear and blue and when he spoke now he looked like a younger man, but wasted and worn down. I can't understand you, she said to him, Carlos, I can't make out what you're saying.

He stopped whispering and stared at her in a mixture of wonder and suspicion. She had spoken in Catalan, and she did not know if that was right: maybe he wanted to talk in Spanish. He gestured to her to come closer. When she brought over a chair beside him he gripped her wrist and the whispering started again, words came and then anxious, heavy breathing. 'Carlos,' she said to him, 'what do you want to say? I'll stay and listen, I swear I'll stay and listen.'

She listened to each word, she listened carefully until she realised what he was asking her, and she understood with horror how difficult it was for him, how desperate he was, and she did not know what to reply. He asked her again, his eyes hard and intent this time. Will I, do you think, am I going to get better, am I going to be normal again, am I going to be all right? The words and phrases came with great difficulty. What do you think?

She told him that every day he was better, that since he came to them he had improved, and soon he would be better, and maybe he would go to Paris, maybe he would find a job there, and they would all help him. After she spoke he was quiet. Later she found him in the same chair, with his eyes closed and his head nodding, and the force of his pain palpable in the room.

*

The police arrived a few days after Michael Graves left. She saw them walking up towards the front door of the house; two of them had machine-guns. Isona was eating at the kitchen table, Carlos Puig was in his room, remote and quiet, Miguel had been out since early morning.

She went to the door to meet them.

'*Dónde está su marido?*'

'*No sé,*' she said. They pushed in past her and found Carlos Puig in the front room. He didn't look up at them, he seemed not to notice that they had come in. She told them he was sick. What was wrong with him, they wanted to know. She pointed to her head and they left the room. They found Isona alone in the kitchen. She looked up at them in wonder, three men entering the kitchen unannounced.

'*Dónde está su marido?*' the oldest one said again. She repeated that she didn't know where her husband was. He asked her what was the name of the man in the other room.

'Carlos Puig,' she said. The man suddenly snorted and laughed. He had his gloves in his hand and he beat them against the leg of his trousers. The other two policemen, both younger, remained serious. Suddenly, Isona began to laugh as well and Katherine went to her and took her in her arms. They left the kitchen and stood in the hall.

'*Dónde está su marido?*' he asked again. This time she didn't answer; when he stared at her, she looked away. He kicked open the door of Carlos Puig's room and let out a loud shout. Carlos Puig looked around at him with a start just as the policeman suddenly turned away to leave.

It was after dark when Miguel came back. She told him what happened, she told him they could put their things in the jeep and go to France, it would take only two hours to get over the border, they could wait until it was late and sneak across. He told her if they left they could never come back.

She told him that she wanted to go. He told her to wait until the morning.

The same three men came in the morning, quite soon after dawn. They would not allow Miguel time to dress himself, they led him out to the jeep; they had handcuffs on Carlos Puig who was already dressed. Carlos Puig looked behind as they walked him down to the police jeep with a look of utter desolation on his face. They pushed him forward with the butt of a gun. In five minutes they had gone. It had happened. She sat in Carlos Puig's chair at the window and caught glimpses of the jeep as it curved its way down. They could have gone by night to France, to Barcelona, to Andorra; they had left it too late.

The jeep had disappeared now. Miguel had no clothes, they had taken him so quickly from the house; she was now on her own with Isona and the villagers who would have witnessed the scene.

There was enough food and there was enough wood. Isona was used to Miguel being away. Katherine took to leaving the child with Fuster's wife in the village and walking for hours in the hills above the house, meeting no one except the foresters, keeping her mind empty.

Miguel needed it to happen here; he could not have gone away. And this she could not understand. She could not fathom why he did not agree to get into the jeep that night with her and Carlos and Isona and flee, leave, never to come back. She could have loved him anywhere. She walked for miles every day to fill in the time before he came back.

She tried to write to her mother and to Michael Graves to tell them that it had gone wrong, that he was taken out of the house in the freezing early morning and that was several weeks ago and she was here on her own with the child. She went no further than composing the letters in her head. She didn't write; she couldn't tell them that she didn't understand something fundamental that had happened here in the mountains.

When she drove to Llavorsi one day to buy supplies, she stopped in the bar to have a coffee. The policeman was there, the older one who had asked her the questions. She did not approach him at first but kept her head down. Only when she ordered a second coffee and took a newspaper from her bag and started to read did she catch his eye, but she looked down again. She drank the coffee and went up to the bar to pay. He turned his back on her.

Outside, she was tempted to go in again and talk to him but she decided instead to go to the police station in the square. A young heavy-set policeman sat at the desk. He did not look up when she approached, although he must have heard her. She stood there for several moments waiting for his attention. Eventually she spoke.

'*Buenos días*,' she said.

'*Buenos días, señora,*' he replied and continued looking at the desk.

'*Qué quiere usted?*' She told him that her husband had been taken from the house three weeks ago, she gave the name and the date. He stood up and walked out past her into the square.

'*Un momento,*' he called back to her.

Boxes with initials on them were stacked neatly against the wall. From above them Generalissimo Franco looked down, proudly, implacably. She heard footsteps and she turned around. The policeman she had seen in the bar was coming towards her followed by the younger man.

He asked for her documents. She reached into her bag and took out her driving licence.

'Where are you from?' he asked.

'I'm Irish,' she said.

'That's a Catholic country, no?'

She hesitated for a moment. 'Yes,' she assented.

'Like Spain,' he said.

'I'm looking for my husband,' she said.

'Yes,' he said.

'Do you know where I can find him?'

'Where is your passport?'

'It's in the house,' she told him.

'Bring it here tomorrow,' he told her.

The following day he was not there, but the younger man told her to wait, that he would be back. She wished to go to the bar and have a coffee but he had instructions to make her wait. The *jefe* said she must wait.

As soon as the *jefe* arrived he asked to see her passport, which she showed him. He disappeared into a back room.

He came out and threw her passport on the table and said she had no right to be in Spain. He stared in anger and she stared back. He picked up the passport again and told her she had to leave.

'My daughter is in the village,' she said.

'So what?'

'I simply want to know where my husband is,' she said.

'He isn't your husband,' he told her.

'Please, I want to know where he is.'

'He is in prison,' he told her.

'Where?'

'In Tremp,' he replied.

'When will he be let out?'

'Now he's in hospital with his friend.'

'Can I visit him?'

'They will be let out next week,' he told her and he walked away. She stood at the desk until it was clear he did not intend to return.

'He has my passport,' she told the man at the desk. He shrugged. She tried to walk past the desk in the wake of the captain but she was stopped.

'*Tiene el pasaporte*,' she repeated.

'*Mañana, puede volver mañana*,' the policeman said.

She did not go back. She waited in the house most of the time, talking to the child, trying to paint on board, watching. The *jefe* had said a week and when a week was up her watching became intense, overwrought. She stood at the window constantly watching for a sign of the jeep, or even a figure on foot. She tried to paint fear, she worked on dark paintings, with figures in the background, faint, ominous figures. All the figures in the foreground were naked, fearful, coiled round one another as though in some hell.

*

He came back late one evening and he talked as though nothing had happened and would not let her look at him closely. He said he was fine. His arm was in a sling. When she went over to him she saw his arm was in plaster. He asked her not to talk. In the morning, he said, they would leave the child in the village and go to Tremp to get Carlos Puig.

She lit another candle so she could see him better. He put his head on the round kitchen table. Again, he asked her not to talk, to leave him, to go to bed. She didn't move. At intervals she could hear him breathe deeply. She asked him if he had eaten and he lifted his head and opened his mouth and pointed into it. His front teeth were broken. '*He mengat els dents,*' he said. He told her to go to bed. Please, he asked her, go to bed. Tomorrow, he said, they would go to Tremp to get Carlos Puig. He repeated this several times. Go to bed, please leave me.

She went upstairs with a candle and lay in the bed knowing that he would not come up. When she took a blanket down and put it around him he did not move, although she knew he was not asleep. She blew the candle out and left him there until the morning.

He had not moved when she came down. She closed the door again and made Isona dress in the bedroom then went down and collected the child's coat. Isona asked if Papa had come back – Katherine told her that he had,

134

but he was tired and would see her later. She took her in her arms and went down to Fuster's house.

In the distance the snow covered only the highest peaks. The sky was clear and blue and a haze lay over the valley as the dew dried on the grass. She stood for a moment and listened to the rush of water all round. The brown stone of the village looked solid and steady now in the morning sunlight. Tremp was three hours away; Carlos Puig was in Tremp; she went into the kitchen and asked if Miguel still wanted to go there. He asked her the time, she told him it was eight in the morning. He told her he wanted to go to bed, she could call him at twelve.

When he stood up she saw him more clearly. His eyes were bloodshot and one eye was bruised and his head had been shaved in several places. He walked with a limp.

She went back to her work. She looked at what she had done, the figures in the foreground looped in terror and anguish and the figure of authority at the back standing erect and supreme. She saw how crude the ideas had been, how bad the painting was. She stacked them into a corner. Later, she would burn them.

He lay in the back of the car on the road to Tremp. He did not speak to her. He brought a cushion and blanket and huddled up. Once beyond Llavorsi the road was flat and easy. After an hour or so she could feel the heat of the summer which had not yet come to the mountains.

She asked him where Carlos Puig was and he told her that he was in a mental hospital.

She asked him why. He didn't answer. She asked him again what was wrong with Carlos Puig but he merely sighed and said he didn't know. He told her the police had broken Carlos Puig's arm with a mallet, and then they had broken his. She asked him whose clothes he was wearing; he told her he had been given clothes in the hospital. Carlos had started to shout and wouldn't stop; he shouted and screamed all night and all day until they moved him. It wasn't loud, but it was a noise everyone could hear. He couldn't do anything except make the noise. He had lost control over his bowels. Miguel tried to talk to him but he didn't seem to hear. Miguel talked to her in a tone that was detached, cold, distant. They were silent for the rest of the journey.

When they arrived in Tremp he told her to take a left turn. For several miles there was nothing except flat fields with cattle and some trees standing alone, but after a while she came to a large clump of pine trees. Miguel was now sitting up in the back of the jeep. He told her he wasn't sure, but he thought she should turn right after the trees. One of the policemen had given him these directions. She could see a building in the distance so when she came to two stone pillars and a gate she got out and opened the gate. There was no sign. Miguel thought this was the mental hospital. She drove through and got out again to close the gate. The avenue was long and the trees grew close in on either side. They drove up to a large grey stone building. Several cars and a van were parked at the side. They could see beds through the windows.

They made their way in by a side door. There was dead silence. The walls were painted a dark brown and there was dark lino on the floor. Religious statues and pictures hung on the walls. When Miguel opened a door at the end of the corridor they found themselves in a long ward, a women's ward. No one noticed them. Some of the women were dressed and moving about, others lay in bed. There was a smell in the ward and Katherine noticed how the blankets and sheets looked stale and dirty. They went back out. At the end of a corridor, they met a nun. Miguel spoke to her and after a while she led them up a few flights of stairs. The nun walked ahead of them and did not speak. There was the same foul smell as there had been in the ward, only muted now by disinfectant. There was still silence everywhere until they reached the top floor. They could hear shouting as they passed a number of doors. They went up a small stairway into an attic. Faint light came from small dormer windows in the roof. The beds were close together. She looked behind as a boy who looked about fifteen or sixteen called out to her and laughed. She smiled at him and he smiled. Further down the ward there were figures in cots with bars over the top making gurgling sounds. Some lay back in the cots, their arms tied to the bars. She couldn't bear to look at them.

The nun walked up the steps into another attic ward and they followed. She saw Carlos Puig immediately. His head was covered in a bandage but she recognised the dead eyes. His hands were tied with bandages to the back of the iron bed. He didn't see them. Miguel talked to him but he didn't respond. Katherine noticed that his teeth were missing. The nun stood at the end of the bed, waiting.

Miguel continued to talk to Carlos Puig but there was

nothing. He told the nun that they wanted to take him home. The nun said he was still in police custody, Miguel would have to go to the police.

They walked out of the hospital. She turned to him and said that they should have gone to France when they had the opportunity, they should have disappeared when they had the chance.

'What will we do with Carlos?' she asked him. He made his way past her and out to the jeep. He lay down in the back with his head on the cushion and closed his eyes.

Autumn

She chopped up the boiled egg on a saucer for Isona. The child sat at the table in her nightdress and took a cup of milk in her hands. It was morning. Miguel was standing at the window with his back to her. 'The snow is coming back. It won't be long.' She spoke in English. '*Qué dius?*' he said. He turned and looked at her suspiciously.

She repeated her words in Catalan. He glanced back at the window and then at her. He didn't speak but turned to the sink and began to stack the dirty dishes neatly. He filled the saucepan with water and put it on the gas. She went and stood at the front door.

It was as though a fire had scorched the valley. Everything was coloured shades of red, or gold, or brown, or rust. She left the child with Miguel, and walked down the road to Tirvia with some paints and paper. She kept her eyes on the valley and watched the way each colour and hint of a colour glittered as it caught the sun. She went back to the house for two chairs – one to sit on, one for the palette and paint.

It was easy to paint. Easier than anything else she could have done. The wood was ready for the winter and there were still a few weeks before the snow. There was nothing else to do except paint.

She needed ten colours: ten shades of rust, red, gold, yellow. And out of each shade she needed to make ten more. Each stroke of the brush had to carry a different colour, each stroke had to be a different size, with a different texture.

All morning the sense of decay impinged as though it were a colour. The paper was good to work on; it was easy to gauge the effect that the paint would have against the white. Also, the paper absorbed nothing, every mark she made stood out and she could test each new shade. But it wasn't enough; she wanted to work on a bigger scale on canvas. She would have to ask Miguel to stretch the canvas for her.

Miguel spent all day with Isona, going to sleep with her in the afternoons, taking her into the wood on his shoulders. When Isona fell or cried, it was Miguel she wanted; or when she woke in the night. She was getting used to being with her father.

Katherine went back to the house and searched in the store until she found some large pieces of wood, a spade and a mallet. She took them back to the hillside and tried to force stakes into the ground to use as an easel. When she discovered that the ground was too hard she went back to the house.

In the kitchen she poured a glass of wine and brought it out on to the balcony. She lit a cigarette and sat down to watch the valley as the sharp light of the afternoon began to fade. She would need the biggest canvas she had ever used for the painting she had in mind. She would have two weeks at least before the snow. She stood up and looked at the scene again before going down to Lidia to collect the milk.

As usual, as every afternoon, Lidia's questions in the cow shed were about Isona and Miguel and were directed at establishing why Katherine did not look after her own daughter.

'Your husband isn't well,' Lidia said to her.

Lidia looked at her carefully from the side of her eyes as she said it, as though it were a threat or an urgent request. She repeated it: '*No está bien tu marido.*' Lidia gave her a bucket of milk and fumbled around the shed for a while before she gave her the change. '*Está muy mal.*' She said it a few more times.

As Katherine turned to go back towards the house she found Lidia's mother standing in the shadows. The old woman was talking but Katherine could not understand her.

Isona was playing on her own in the garden. Katherine picked her up and took her into the house. Miguel was in the kitchen. Katherine put Isona down. There was hot water on the gas; she washed out the jug and poured in the milk from the bucket.

She asked Miguel to take the bucket back to Lidia. He was taking off Isona's shoes and he looked up. She left the bucket on the table. 'Down in the cow shed they say you're not well,' she said to him in Catalan. 'I'm fed up listening to them.'

He didn't reply.

She asked him to stretch and treat a big canvas for her. Later, he said, later, he would do it later. They still had

141

to eat and put the child to bed. Miguel seemed down-hearted, dispirited. His depression had not lifted for weeks.

*

When he had put Isona to bed he took the lantern down to the store. He asked Katherine what size she wanted the canvas. Big, she said, big. Maybe three metres long and two wide. He went down to the floor below where the wood was kept and he came up with several long planks. All day she had watched the valley as though it were a painting and now she sat and watched him work by the weak light of the lantern in the fusty, untidy room with its dirty, uneven floorboards. That, too, could be a painting. She was aware that she had begun to observe each thing as though it were a scene, as though she needed to fix it in her memory, as if she might never get a chance to see it again. He was still thin, even thinner than almost ten years ago when she had first met him. His hair was still thick and dark. He loved making things, using his hands. He worked quickly, with extraordinary dexterity.

She went over to some painted canvases resting against a wall. She found a number of small canvases packed in against one another. With one hand she held the outer ones and with the other she picked out one of the paintings nearest the wall and took it over to the light.

It was a still life: a dead rabbit hanging upside down, with potatoes, carrots, peppers, garlic, tomatoes on a shelf. The background was dark and the light came from behind the painter. She liked the painting and wondered why she had never seen it before.

Miguel was nailing two planks together. She showed him the still life and asked whose it was. He continued working for a time and ignored her question, then he stood up and walked towards her. He took it up and held it against the light. 'It's mine,' he said. 'When I used to be a painter.' Miguel put the painting back exactly where it had been against the wall.

*

In the bedroom she closed the shutters of the window. She took off her clothes and stood there in the candlelight looking at herself in the mirror: a naked woman in a dim candlelit room; a naked woman of more than forty. In the background a large double bed with blankets pulled back as though waiting for someone to get in. An old tin candlestick with the stub of a candle.

She put her arms into the white nightgown first and then pulled it over her head. He always slept naked. Sometimes he wore a scarf, a short silk scarf around his neck to save himself from sore throats. Less and less he kissed her mouth. His hands became the conductor between his desire and hers. His hands moved over her incessantly. He kept his head buried in the pillow behind her shoulder and he put his hands everywhere he wanted. He used his hands to make his penis hard. And when that was ready he tested her for wetness with his finger and then he pushed his penis inside and began to move it in and out.

Sometimes he would get her legs and put them around

his back. Sometimes he would move his penis in a sort of circular motion. Always he wanted to be finished quickly and, being an expert in all things physical, in lighting fires, chopping wood, stretching canvas, he knew how to reach orgasm quickly. He no longer cared whether she did or not.

In the morning she went down to the hillside where she had tried to stake an easel. She took only a pencil and a sketch pad. Miguel had left Isona with Fuster's wife in the village and was busy stretching her canvas. He told her he would put the stakes in the ground for her.

She took a section of the landscape which included Tirvia, the valley, the distant mountains and the sky, and marked it out on the paper. She divided it into twelve sections and tried to work out what she wanted to do.

By afternoon Miguel had the canvas ready and he carried it down. Isona followed him, intrigued by the canvas and the stakes. Miguel was distant with Katherine but seemed concerned that she approved of the work he had done. She held Isona's hand as Miguel hammered the stakes into the ground.

'Your mama's going to do a painting,' she said. Isona smiled at her first and then laughed. '*El Papa em porta al bosc*,' she said. 'Which wood?' Katherine asked in English. '*Cap àlla*,' she pointed. 'And what are you going to do in the wood?' Katherine asked her. '*El Papa em conta histories*,' the child said. 'Which stories?' Katherine asked. '*La historia del llop que viu al bosc*.' Miguel heard and turned around and growled. It was a game. Katherine watched him with relief. Maybe he was getting better. His front teeth, all except one, were missing. Isona ran to her mother as though she were afraid and when Katherine took her up in her arms she laughed.

When they had left she divided the canvas as she had the paper. She sat for a while and observed the valley and the range of colours in the valley. She noticed how exact each colour was. She narrowed her eyes so as not to focus them on anything.

She began at the top working at first with the pencil on paper to sketch what she planned to paint. She waited until four in the afternoon until the glare had gone from the sun before she began to paint. She had plotted only the lines and the direction of the brush strokes, but not the colours. She stood on the chair and began the colours, sometimes letting the drips run and other times wiping them away.

She was absorbed in the paint when she heard Lidia calling her name. She was tired of Lidia. Lidia was running towards her but she decided to keep painting and ignore her, to let her know that she was not concerned about her shouting. She grew louder, however. 'It's Miguel,' she shouted in Spanish, 'He's in the kitchen. He's burning things. And the child is crying.'

Katherine got down from the chair and walked slowly towards the house.

'*Gracias*, Lidia,' she said, turning slowly around and making sure that the sarcasm in her voice was clear.

The child was indeed crying. She could hear the child crying. She walked quickly into the kitchen which was full of smoke, some of it thick and black. Pieces of canvas had fallen from the grate and were burning on the floor. Isona was hysterical.

Miguel had smashed the glass on some of the paintings and torn the canvases and broken the wood of the frames. Then he had thrown everything into the fire. He seemed not to notice her as she entered the room.

Since there was nothing she could do to stop him she took Isona sobbing in her arms and went out of the room, leaving him to destroy what was left to destroy.

Tirvia

During the time she worked on these paintings she left the child with Fuster's wife in the morning before she and Miguel carried the canvas down and rested it on the staked easel.

Miguel looked after Isona in the afternoon. By the time it was important, by the time the dead light of late afternoon appeared, Katherine was alone there working, trying to follow the plans she had made for the paint.

Michael Graves wrote as she knew he would, and said he would come as she had asked. She said nothing to Miguel before she drove down to meet Michael Graves from the bus. Now she would have to start rationalising, excusing, explaining. Now that she had asked him to come she would have to talk to him and listen to him.

Before the bus arrived she bought some bread and flour and fruit. She put these in the jeep. The bus was always late, and she sat in the bar drinking coffee.

There were two policemen in the bar. She had learned not to look at them or speak to them. She sat with her back to them.

*

When the bus arrived she went out and searched for Michael Graves and when she saw him she was surprised how pleased she was to see him. They went into the bar and she hugged him, ignoring the policemen once more.

'How is he? Is there something wrong?' Michael Graves asked her.

'I think he is very bad. I want you to tell me how bad he is.'

They set off in silence. After the first curve on the dirt track they began to drive along the rim of the valley. Suddenly, the autumn colours filled up all the landscape in front of them. Down the ridge and along the valley basin for miles were the yellows, browns, golds of decay.

'I wish I knew I could spend the rest of my life here,' she said.

'Why can't you?' he asked.

'I always feel that I have just borrowed it for a few years. I watch it all the time because I will need to remember it. Maybe that's why I'm painting it.'

'What's wrong with Miguel?' he asked.

'If I tell you what I think is wrong with him and then tell you that I leave him on his own with Isona every day, you will think there is something wrong with me and not with him. Actually, I don't know what's wrong with him.'

She stopped the jeep when they came to the canvas which she had left resting against the stakes. It was almost finished and the unfinished sections appeared deliberate.

The painting looked as though it had been drowned in a faded gold. The precise delineations of the valley had been carefully, almost academically included, but what caught the eye was the colour and then the detail within the colour.

'It's only half done. I've finished three others. I think this is the best,' she said.

'It's very strong,' he said.

'You don't like it?' she asked.

'Like it? It's not the sort of thing I would do, but I think it's very good,' he said.

He sat down on the rug beside her and kissed her neck.

'I was glad when you wrote,' he said.

She wasn't paying attention. Her eye had fixed on a point across the valley.

'There! Can you see? Look!' she tried to make him see.

'Can you not see?' she said. 'It's them.'

'What's wrong?' Michael Graves asked her. 'I can't see anything wrong.'

'Can you not see them?' she asked.

'I can see someone's there, but I can't see anything wrong.'

'Can't you see that Miguel has Isona with him?'

'Katherine, what's wrong? What's the problem? Please tell me what's wrong.'

She did not answer for a while. She stood watching and then went back to the rug and sat down.

'I don't know,' she said. She closed her eyes.

'I know you don't understand. Since Carlos Puig died, since the day we brought him up here in a coffin, in the back of the jeep and buried him across there in Alendo – something I thought I would never have to go through in my life – I've been afraid. Since that time things have just fallen apart. You don't know what it's been like. We opened the coffin in the house. I don't know why we did that. We had seen the body already, in the hospital. Miguel held Carlos's hands until we shut the coffin again and brought him over to Alendo in the jeep.'

'Maybe we should go on to the house,' he said.

'We'll drive up and come back down for the painting. I don't want it out all night,' she said.

'Does Miguel know I'm here?' he asked.

'No.'

'Didn't you tell him I was coming?'

Katherine started the jeep before she spoke: 'I know you are going to think that there is more wrong with me than there is with Miguel. I want to assure you that you would be very wrong to think that.'

'Are you going to leave?' he asked her.

'I don't know.'

'Why not take Isona down to Barcelona for a few days just to let things settle?'

'Nothing will settle.'

'Are you having problems with Miguel?'

'Do you know how long it is since I have talked to him?'

'Tell me.'

'It's several months.'

'Then leave for a while. It's so isolated here it would drive anyone out of their minds. Come down.'

'I don't know.'

'Why are you so worried about Isona being with Miguel?'

'I think he has fixed on her in some way. I can't talk about this without sounding ludicrous.'

*

They had taken in the painting and collected the milk from Lidia by the time Miguel returned with Isona asleep in his arms. Isona cried as soon as he let her down. Miguel embraced Michael Graves and addressed him in Catalan which Michael could not understand. Miguel started to talk with the local accent of the villagers, especially when he saw that Michael had brought several bottles of brandy. Isona laughed at Miguel's Catalan.

After dinner Miguel drank a large glass of brandy in one swill, slammed his two hands on the table, stood up and took the child in his arms. Katherine asked him where he was going. He told her he was going to leave the child with Fuster's wife so that they could go to the bar in Tirvia. She asked Michael Graves if he wanted to go, but Miguel had already left before he could answer.

'Do you want to go?' Michael Graves asked her.

'Do you?'

'I'll do anything, Katherine. He seems very well. Maybe it's just a first impression and it's wrong, but he seems very well.'

'Yes it is a first impression and it is wrong. On the other hand, maybe there is something wrong with me. Maybe it's me you should watch carefully.'

Miguel didn't want her to take the jeep. He wanted them to walk the four kilometres to Tirvia. There was no moon and only at certain points of the road could the lights of a village be seen. Sometimes it was impossible to see ahead. She could sense that Michael Graves was afraid so she stayed close to him. He complained of the cold. She could feel that snow was on its way and it would only be a matter of days before winter would set in.

There was no bar in Tirvia, merely a house that served drink in the kitchen. There were a few local men there already drinking. They sat on a bench on the other side of the room and ordered hot brandy. Several of the men came over and shook their hands, remembering Michael Graves from a previous visit, when he had spent the night singing. '*Canta molt bé l'irlandès,*' one of them said. The men talked among themselves for a while, then one came back over and asked Michael Graves to sing. Michael told her to tell the man that he was too cold to sing but he would sing later. Katherine asked the man if he could sing and he said that years ago he used to sing but now he didn't. Years ago, before the war.

Miguel turned to Michael Graves and said everything happened years ago, before the war. Now nothing happened. They used to make their own flour before the war. Now there was nothing, no life. He went to the window and looked out.

Michael Graves sang *The Lass of Aughrim* and there was silence.

She watched Miguel but he gave no sign that he was paying attention to the song. When Michael Graves finished, there was applause from the men and Miguel went across the room to order more drink. One of the men started a song in Catalan.

*

She stood at the door with her coat on waiting for them to finish their drinks and come home with her.

'There's brandy at home. Come on.'

They didn't want to go. It was always like this when they had more than a few drinks. They would warm to each other and want to stay talking and singing all night. She walked back to the window where Miguel had stood earlier in the evening; by the few lights left on in the village she could see stars of frost on the road.

They moved out into the cold to begin the long climb to the house. At first it was difficult to see anything in the dark. Michael Graves asked them to stop until his eyes adjusted to the absence of light. They stood and listened to the small noises: the rush of water, the wind, their breathing. 'Let's go,' Michael Graves said and she held his hand for a while as they walked along.

After several minutes Katherine realised that Miguel was not with them, that he must have lingered. She called. There was no reply. She called again. Her voice came back as an echo. She let Michael's hand go and retraced her steps a little. Michael followed. She told him to remain completely quiet. She stood still. She could hear no third presence, no one else's breath. 'Miguel,' she called again. Suddenly, she could feel him close by her, felt as though he were watching her in the dark. She found herself clutching Michael Graves.

'What is it?'

'I feel he's standing here, near us.'

'He's not. He couldn't be.'

They stood together, saying nothing.

'Maybe he went on ahead,' Michael Graves said. 'Maybe if we go fast we'll catch up with him.' He began to walk on and she followed. She was afraid.

*

Miguel did not appear during the night and when she woke in the morning it took her a moment to realise that the sound that woke her was her own sound, that she had cried out with whatever pain had filled her dream.

She lay for a while and watched the full-bodied light of the morning.

The sun was well up. She took in every object in the room. She began to conjure up Enniscorthy, her last year at home, how they had gone out in the old Morris Oxford on a Sunday afternoon to Blackwater. It must have been November or December and she remembered that the sky was a sheer ice blue without a trace of cloud and the day was calm, as though winter was over and spring had come. They walked down by the river, Tom, herself and Richard, along what they took to be a right-of-way. They passed an old ruin and later they crossed a footbridge to where there was a small whitewashed cottage.

She remembered that Tom had wanted to turn back; he thought they might be trespassing, but Richard wanted to go on and so did she. The house was well kept; there were roses in front, or maybe other red flowers, or maybe the galvanised roof was painted red. Tom insisted on going back.

They had not noticed the other people out walking, and she did not recognise the man coming towards them until he spoke and she remembered him as the man who had painted the downstairs rooms of the house for them. He said it was a fine day.

'Yes,' she said. 'It is like a day in spring.'

'It's a nice place for a walk,' he said.

'Yes, it is nice,' she replied. Tom said nothing.

'You'd feel sorry for them inside,' the man said and pointed at the house. Tom left them and walked on ahead without a word but Richard and she stood while the man continued.

'Poor things. We were just saying it was awful,' the man's wife said.

'Once it gets into a house, that's the end then,' the man added. Katherine could see Tom was waiting for them to finish the conversation. Tom did not mix with Catholics.

'Sorry, I don't know what you mean,' she said.

'The TB,' the man said, 'all four daughters dead with it. The four of them gone. She's no one left now, the mother.'

'I don't understand,' Katherine said.

'The last of them was buried – when would it be? – just two weeks ago last Friday,' he continued.

'What happened to them?' Katherine asked. 'How did they all die?'

'The TB, tuberculosis,' the man said, 'it's ruined nearly the whole country.' He began to move away. 'Good day to you now,' he said.

'Goodbye,' Katherine said and she and Richard joined Tom who was waiting for them.

*

Katherine was worried about the silence, about where Miguel had gone. Maybe Miguel was in the house and he would come if she called out.

How sharp Enniscorthy still was in her mind as she lay in bed. How precise her memory now of the hills in the town, of the greenness of the grass around the Protestant church, of the bracken trapped at the parapets of the bridge. Of the fire blazing in the reading room of the Atheneum and the long wooden table with its carved legs, the table full of newspapers and magazines. Of the map of the county on the wall, its faded yellowish colours and the huge mouth of the Slaney, which was now filled up on newer maps. The billiard room at the back where the silence was even more sacred than in the reading room, the green baize and the huge light over the table.

*

When she heard footsteps in the hall, she was sure Miguel had come back. She felt suddenly relieved, almost happy. But when the door of the bedroom opened, she saw that it was Michael Graves.

'Has he come back?' she asked.

'I haven't seen him,' he said.

'He must have stayed out all night. I thought that he would have arrived back before us last night. I wonder where he is.'

'Have you been awake long?' he asked.

'I've been awake all morning.'

'I've only just woken up,' he said.

'You've slept right through the morning. We should really go down and collect Isona.'

'No, it's early still. I don't think that Lidia has taken in the cows yet.'

'Of course she has. She brought them in four or five hours ago. Look at the light.'

'It's not eight o'clock yet,' he said.

'I don't believe you.'

'My watch says five to eight.'

'It's wrong, it's past midday. I've been awake for hours.'

'No, my watch hasn't stopped. That's really the time.' He went into the kitchen and brought in the clock. It was five to eight.

'I've misunderstood everything then, haven't I?' she said. 'Haven't I?'

Miguel

He was missing. She believed that he was close by. She stood at the big window in the long room, the spot from which she had watched the first snow, and looked out. The valley in autumn. He was another being amongst all the life out there, a small element, as important as a tree in the great sweep of things. Neither his consciousness nor hers were of any significance. Her love for him, she thought, was another small pattern of grief and happiness. Her love for him was like breath on glass.

She left Isona with Fuster's wife and told her that Miguel had gone to Barcelona. Then she took Michael Graves to the small graveyard on the promontory at Alendo where Carlos Puig was buried.

They sat down in the graveyard and looked on to the valley and the village. Michael Graves took out the new binoculars he had brought with him and searched the valley. Eventually he asked: 'Are you going to come down with me?'

'I don't know,' she said.

'Come now, today, let's just get into the jeep and go,' he said.

'Go where?'

159

'Barcelona.'

'I don't know what to do. He was fine last night. He was in good form when he saw you.'

'Leave him for a while.'

'I've done that before.'

'Was it a good decision?'

'Wonderful, wonderful thing to do, leave a father with his ten-year-old son,' she laughed.

'Was it a bad thing then?'

'Yes, of course it was bad.'

'This is different though.'

'Leave me alone, Michael. Don't give me advice.'

'Let's go now,' he said.

'I want you to know that I will never leave Miguel.'

'Leave him a note saying that you've gone to Barcelona with Isona for a few days.'

'What? Pinned to the door?'

'On the table.'

'I don't know.'

'It's not as though you're leaving him for good.'

'Do you think I could come back?'

'I think you should both leave here.'

'Don't say that.'

'Have you got your passport back?'

'No, but I've written to the embassy in Madrid telling them I lost it. I sent them Isona's birth certificate as well, so she'll be on my passport.'

'You can ring them from Barcelona.'

Michael Graves had leaned back and was staring at the sky. He suddenly sat up.

'Is that your jeep?' he asked, and she listened for the

sound of the engine, but heard nothing at first. Then from the village she heard it and knew it was her jeep.

'Is it your jeep?' he repeated.

'Yes, but I can't think who is driving,' she said. The revving became louder as though the jeep was stuck in the wrong gear. She was puzzled.

'It might be the milk jeep, I'm not sure.' They heard the jeep moving off, but it still sounded as though it was in the wrong gear.

'It's someone who can't drive,' Michael said as they stood up.

When the jeep came into view she knew it was hers. She reached for the binoculars, but Michael wouldn't let her have them.

'It's Miguel driving, isn't it? Let me have them.' She snatched the glasses from him. Through them she could see Miguel's face clearly.

'He can't drive,' she said, staring across.

'Who else is in the jeep?' Michael asked.

'No one. It's just him.'

'Give me the glasses,' he insisted. She handed him the binoculars.

'There's someone else in the jeep,' he said and then let out a cry. 'Oh Jesus!'

Again she took the glasses from him, but had difficulty focusing, finding the jeep. Then she found it. 'He's got Isona in the car. He has her on the front seat.'

'Run,' Michael said. 'We should try and get to them.' She handed him back the binoculars.

She could not move. She heard the gears grinding.

'Oh God,' she said, 'let this be all right. Let this be all right.' She willed Miguel to find the first gear.

'Come on,' Michael said. 'Let's get over there.'

She knew how easily the gears slipped. She knew, too, how stubborn Miguel was, how he hated giving up.

'They're going to crash, they're going to go down.' At that moment the jeep lurched back to the edge of the track. It went over, tumbling and somersaulting. Within a few seconds it was lying at the bottom of the steep incline, leaving a trail of dust and loose stones in its wake.

Michael Graves was already running ahead, shouting back at her. She looked down at the stillness, below, where the jeep had settled. She heard him shouting at her to follow, but she could not move.

PART TWO

Barcelona: 1964

Miguel, five years dead, I am in Barcelona now. Last evening the swifts came back to the city. I remember how we sat one evening as the sky darkened and stared at them frantic in the air above Calle Carmen. We had been drinking. I remember it. The swifts frantic in the air.

I am watching them now, Miguel. They fly into the gaps in the stone of the houses in the Barrio Gótico. I am the woman at the window with the chair half out on the balcony, the cane chair with the footrest which I rescued from a rubbish heap on Calle Ancha.

The swifts criss-cross over Calle Condesa Sobradiel.

Every morning now I walk up to Plaza Regomir, just as the children are being led to school. I go to a café there. I sit looking out on to the plaza.

Miguel, I am in Barcelona now. At night the blare of the fog horn comes up here from the port. I sleep in the front room when I am low. I like the noise at night, the shouts in the street, the conversations going on beneath the window, a taxi roaring by. I often switch on the light and try to read but I can't concentrate. At first light, five or maybe six – it depends – I dress and go out. I walk up to Calle Fernando and then to Plaza San Jaime. In the faded grey light I walk through the Barrio Gótico. I sit in Felipe Neri where we used to sit. I walk down Santa Eulalia to Baños Nuevos, into Plaza del Pino, along Petritxol to the Ramblas.

They are used to me in the markets. The men bringing in produce from the country don't even comment now. Two of the bars there open early and I will drink coffee if I know that there is no chance of going back to sleep.

Once, it must have been in the back room of someone's flat, we had been together some time, I'm not sure how long, but a year, it was certainly a year. It was not a familiar room, I woke to find your arms around me. It was as though we had been touching each other for a long time. We made love over and over for the rest of the night with small snatches of sleep in between. We were locked in each other's arms. This had never happened before and would never happen again with such intensity.

Every night after you were killed I took sleeping pills. Two, I was told, never take more than two, be careful. And I did as they said. Never more than two.

Miguel, my battle now is with sleep. Now that I don't want pills, I have no control over the tides of sleep which ebb and flow. For weeks I haunt the markets and Barrio Gótico. For weeks I lie in the dark in the front room of this flat in Calle Aviño and hear every noise. I can do nothing all day; I am weak and can't concentrate.

And then it stops: the sleep wells up slowly like blood from a cut and I try to hold it. I move into the back room, into the thick air of the room with no window and I sleep all night.

Miguel, I am the woman who wanders about inside the port as the daylight goes, carrying a canvas, an easel and oils. This is my work now. As the day wanes I paint the port of Barcelona. I paint the sound of the fog horn and the fog. The warehouses, cranes, containers. I paint trade.

How could I explain to those two men in the port authority? The office was all polished wood and brass, full of the smell of old papers piled up everywhere: permits for goods going to Valencia, Marseilles, Genoa, New York. And the two men listening to me at the other side of the desk and me showing them the catalogue of my exhibition and trying to explain why I wanted to paint the port.

They could see nothing there for a painter. They felt that I should go to the coast like Sunyer – they used his name – or to the mountains like Miró. A port was not for painting. A port was ugly, oily, smelly. I told them I had already been to the mountains and the sea. One of the Catalans was brown, with a small greying moustache. He frowned. I said you must let me, you can lose nothing. He nodded his head, the brown one. '*Bueno,*' he said, '*si vol vosté pintar el port . . .*' and shrugged his shoulders. I took it to be an agreement and thanked them both. I asked for a letter that would give me access to the port at all times.

I went at twilight to paint the light; the objects stayed in the background. Everything muted, faded, about to be subsumed into the night. It is the most mysterious place in the whole world. Cargoes arrive and are held for a day on the wharf or in a warehouse and then moved; ships dock and more goods are taken on and off; the port buildings are vast and beautiful. I paint what is transient as it pulses faintly in the light.

All the work has been dull recently: I have dulled every colour. Now I have started painting sections of the port on small square canvases.

*

Listen Miguel, Ramon Rogent is dead. I saw him every day when I came back here first. Ramon and Montserrat made me stay. Ramon was driving, he was a good driver. I don't know why he was killed.

All my grief came back. I re-lived your death. I wondered how the next day would go, would I still have to brood for hours, would I still want you back in the room now, want to make love, to go around the bars with you?

It is impossible, despite the fact that you have died and that I will die too, despite the fact that I often suffer from intense loneliness here, it is impossible not to consider the miracle of being alive, of watching the swifts skirting the air just before night falls, the old man moving up Calle Condesa Sobradiel – the gift of consciousness, the life still left in me.

I can turn my head now and gaze over at the painting I bought from Ramon Rogent – *The Hammock*. All the techniques he learned from Dufy and Matisse are there, but in the colours of the woman's dress, the sheer luxury of the paint, there is Ramon. Ramon curling his lip to smile with his thin face. I have that painting as a symbol of joy in this room.

I work hard sometimes. I live with paint and delight in the pleasure it gives. It feels as though it were clay I was plastering across the canvas with the brush or with my fingers, it feels like some essential element. I leave the picture there to rest and settle and I return then to see how it looks when the experience of doing it is over, when it is merely what is left of a certain time, when it adds to the store of things.

There are friends: other lives to brush against. But there will be no new intimacies like the old ones. There will always be reservations, things one must leave out, events one can't explain without handing over a full map of one's life, unfolding it, making clear that all the lines and contours stand for long days and nights when things were bad, or good, or when things were too small to be described at all: when things just were. This is a life.

I go to the Palau de la Música. Sometimes when I walk into the hall and up the main stairs I see it again as I did that first year in Barcelona. The colours and the motifs distract from the music, it is overdone. But sometimes when the lights go down and you watch the stage, you can sense the splendour of the whole building.

I go with a Catalan friend Maria Jover, whose eyes still fill with tears when she talks about the civil war. I like her softness and her prejudice. I go to her house on Saturday for lunch. Her daughter is there sometimes and they like to talk about culture: an exhibition, a concert, old Barcelona, books. Maria Jover was able to show me a catalogue for a show that you were in nearly twenty years ago.

It took me a while to tell her about you. At first I mentioned that I had known you and I saw her watching me and it was some weeks before she mentioned that she knew you had gone to the Pyrenees to live with *una anglesa* and I said yes that I had lived with you and that I was there when you were killed and that I had a daughter with you and she died in the accident as well and I was heartbroken at the loss of both of you.

We talk a lot about painters and paintings. She lives down by the side of Santa Maria del Mar. Her husband, too, was held after the civil war. She has not told me about what happened to him – yet I want to know why he was never able to work again. He did not die until recently. Maria gives the impression, however, that he died long ago. I have never asked her too many questions about it. Yet his presence and yours hang over our conversation. When we go to a concert together it is as though we should keep two seats vacant, one for you and one for her husband who was tortured after the civil war. For both of us reality rests in being reminded. For me the whole city of Barcelona, every street I use, every day, evokes memories of the years we were together.

Last week Maria and I came out after a concert in the Palau. We did not speak, we often stay silent as we walk out. We had been listening to Bach's cello suites. There was just the single instrument. I was moved by the music. Maria said she had heard Casals playing the Bach in Prades. The music had made me low. I could not face the night on my own trying to sleep.

I asked her to come for a drink. I don't think she wanted to. I was tired of being alone. She said she would drink a cup of coffee but she sounded reluctant. I took her to the Meson del Café where you would go to wait for me and Michael Graves after the first half of a concert, to wait for me and Michael Graves when you had finished looking at the stained glass on the ceiling and the Catalan girls. You had no time for the music then.

I sat there with her. I ordered a brandy with my coffee. She was uncomfortable in the bar. She doesn't go to bars and she knows nothing of my life that I do not tell her. I talked about the last year of our life together. I told her about Carlos Puig.

I did not tell her how you died or how Isona died. I know that you were driving a jeep and the jeep reversed off the road just outside the village. I know Isona was in the front seat and I know she broke her neck. I am told, they tell me, that she died instantly. They tell me too that you were still alive when they got to you. No one has ever told me if you said anything and I have never asked. I have always presumed that you were too badly injured to talk but maybe you could open your eyes, maybe you could hear. I can't fill in those bits. I do not know what you felt. I had ceased to understand what you felt sometime before.

There is one thing. I cannot contemplate what happened when the jeep went off the road, those moments. I must not contemplate what happened when the jeep went off the road. Did Isona scream? Miguel, what did she do, the poor child? Miguel, I am in Barcelona now.

I cannot think about what happened. It is something I stop myself doing at all hours of the day and night.

I can feel you close.

I told Maria that I had to stop myself thinking about that. I did not tell her that you wanted to kill yourself and to kill the child. Nor did I imply it. I said it was an accident. I said you couldn't drive. I said maybe you got into the wrong gear. I said the roads were bad. I said whatever I could. I told her the drop was sheer. I do not know what happened. I had lost touch with you. You had disappeared. I do not even know how you managed to start the jeep.

Maria also has a man to remember. I do not know what they did to him. I do not know which method they used to unnerve him. She knows what happened; it was public; she has the motives in her possession. I do not. I thus cannot judge. There are facts missing.

Don't move. Hold still. I can feel you close.

It is late spring in Barcelona, nearly summer. The swifts are frantic in the air. I am the woman at the window with the chair half out on the balcony, the cane chair with the footrest that I rescued from a rubbish heap in Calle Ancha.

I am lingering here without knowing what to do. And Michael Graves still wants me after all this time. His failure in everything has become for him his failure with me. He has failed to persuade me to live with him, he has failed to make me believe that he can look after me.

I will not settle for him.

There are times when I have wanted to. I needed someone, I needed a set of domestic circumstances, someone to talk to, share meals with, make love to, go out to the bars with. I have never made love with him, although I have sometimes wanted to; even years ago when I was with you I wanted to. Maybe if I had made love with him then things would be different.

I didn't make love with him then.

I doubt if sex matters to either of us any more.

Loneliness, the loss of energy, selfishness, insomnia, these are some of my problems. He drinks too much, he works too little, he needs me too badly for me to be able to take him. I am not in love with Michael Graves, that is the answer. I cannot live with him, I have nothing to offer him, I cannot look after him, I cannot be the focus of all his hope. I want him to go away. I want you back.

I want you back. That is what I want.

I see him as often as I can. He is still funny and good-humoured and he still loves Barcelona. It is a relief to see him. I must keep him at arm's length.

He wants me to come back with him to Dublin. He says I cannot remain here forever brooding about you. He says I must move, even if to London or anywhere outside Spain. Maybe it is time I abandoned all this.

*

I went to Ireland with him last year. I did not go to Enniscorthy and I lived in fear that someone might recognise me. In the streets of Dublin I constantly saw people I thought I knew. I kept watching them and they would turn out to be someone else, someone I didn't know.

We went to Hook Head for a week. We hired a car and drove from Dublin. We passed through Wexford as the April day was fading and drove towards the sea. There was a guarded pink light which covered everything. We drove towards the sea at dusk, Michael and I, gazing at the extraordinary light. Neither of us had ever seen it before, although we were both born just thirty miles away. It was like being in another country. When we came to the first inlet we stopped to watch. Everything was governed by this light. Everything was changed by it.

We were on Hook Head with the sea on three sides. This is the Ireland I imagined you and me being furtive in. Staying in the small places as husband and wife. I almost loved Michael Graves that night.

I shall leave here; I shall give up longing for you. I must leave you dead, leave you buried in Alendo in the graveyard, the first bodies to be buried there in years, under the marble gravestone I brought up from Barcelona. You and Isona and poor Carlos Puig, whose body lies beside yours.

There is still only one matter which will keep hammering away in my mind and it is what happened in the jeep when it went off the road. What went through your mind? What about Isona? Did you know what you were doing? Why did you take her?

This is what you have left me with: anguish, speculations, doubts. Over and over again. Help me. Miguel, listen to me. I am in Barcelona now. Last evening the swifts came back to the city. I remember how we sat one evening as the sky darkened and stared up at them frantic in the air above Calle Carmen. We had been drinking. I remember it. The swifts frantic in the air.

Dublin in Winter

Dublin in winter. In November the sky was an intense, cold grey; the light was clear and brittle. In December the darkness almost never left the sky; the day was an interlude.

Fog seeped everywhere in January. In the little warren of houses around Oxmanstown Road where she moved when she returned to Ireland, the smoke from the chimneys didn't lift, it hung heavy in the air all day. There was ice on the footpaths in the morning; there was a damp and bitter cold.

Michael Graves telephoned her every morning and came across the city twice or three times a week. Sometimes they drank until closing time in Mulligan's pub in Stoneybatter; some nights she cooked for him, but she was a bad cook.

This was her second winter. She rarely travelled far beyond the few streets around her house. The weather reminded her of an impression she had once had of death. To be enveloped thus in a casual, alien cold.

She could think of nothing to do. Everything she touched was damp; every night the sheets on the bed were damp, no matter how long she left the electric blanket on. The walls were damp. She could feel the damp everywhere; she could feel the damp in the clothes she was wearing.

There were two upstairs rooms in the house. The front room was full of her stores: old paintings, half finished paintings. She tried to stay in bed in the morning. She tried to paint when she got up. Michael Graves gave her books. Sometimes there was music on the radio and that was good.

The front room downstairs had a sofa where Michael Graves slept when he stayed. He was as lonely as she, even though he had his pubs, his friends, and a pattern to his life in the city. He hardly ever painted, only when commissioned, and even then he was slow and cranky. He lived on the dole which he collected every week. He complained about money, he complained about the cost of his flat. He wanted to move in with her.

She cared for him. Perhaps loved him. She needed him at the other side of the city, as a visitor, as a constant companion.

A Letter from Faro

Hotel Eva
Faro
Portugal
May 8 1971

Michael Graves my love,

As you will have seen from the notepaper and the stamp on the envelope we are not in Venice as we were meant to be. This may come as a surprise to you and I can assure you it came as a surprise to me when we arrived at the airport in London and mother produced the tickets. You will note from the date above that one week has gone and there are five more to go.

We fill three rooms of the Hotel Eva. Mother and I each have a bedroom with bathroom en suite; between our rooms there is another room with a dining table and some easy chairs, each room has a balcony looking out on to a small marina. It is, as mother says, 'much nicer than Venice – isn't it dear? – much nicer than Venice.'

Mother has become larger than life. She was never small, but for this holiday she seems to have modelled herself on a number of well-known figures from the cinema. She has brought a lot of Henry James's novels.

We have breakfast at eight in our dining room. Mother demands that I be dressed before she starts. She knows about you, or at least she knows a certain amount about you. She asked me where you came from. I told her. She looked at me. Enniscorthy, she said, that's where we're from. Yes, I said, I know. 'What's his name again?' she asked and repeated it slowly. 'Did he have a grandfather called Michael Graves?' I said I didn't know. (Do you? If you do, send me a telegram.)

She remembered a man called Michael Graves well. He was tall. Were you tall? (Are you tall?) She remembered he was the only man in Enniscorthy at the turn of the century who could sign his name. 'The rest of them just wrote X my dear, imagine that.' She looked at me daring me to say that I didn't believe her. Then she added: 'He is RC, isn't he?' I said yes. That was a week ago, our first day on the beach and since then she has been chuckling to herself: 'My daughter is going out with a boy from the town, an RC.' She repeats it four or five times a day and I don't think that she is going to stop.

I have a lot of time on my hands. I hope you don't mind if I ramble on for a while. Last night my mother looked out of the window and saw the town. 'Oh,' she said, 'there's a town as well as a beach. A town. I hope you won't be thinking now of going out with any of the boys, my dear.' I looked up from my book. 'I am too old for boys.' There was silence for a while. Then she said: 'Yes, so am I.' She is almost eighty.

There is the ceremony known as moving mother to the beach. There is no beach in the town and she knew that before she came. The beach is two miles across a lagoon. Mother loves saying the word lagoon. 'There's a lagoon, my dear, just like in Venice.' The hotel provides a motorboat and a boatman. Mother must first be moved from her room, all hats, sunglasses, scarves, necklaces and Henry James novels. Then she has to be helped out of the lift and into the boat. The boat must also contain an armchair and a footrest as well as a table for her use on the beach. The boatman, or, as she calls him, the ferryman, is in charge of the furniture. She comments on everything that happens. 'Now we are ready,' she will say, 'for the ferryman to take us across the lagoon.' Or: 'Halfway there, my dear, halfway there.' The boatman must then carry all the furniture to a *toldo* and then get mother and seat her in the shade, with her feet on the footrest, her sunhat on her head and her Henry James on the table. She will also have organised a small hamper and a tip for the ferryman who took her across the lagoon. A tip for the ferryman! I am not joking.

From then on it's advice, comment, gossip, reminiscences. Nothing she tells me is true, or maybe some of it is true, but not much of it. Every time I sit in the sun, she croaks at me and tells me it will ruin my skin. Never sit in the sun. She says it five times a day. Never sit in the sun. One day she moved her glasses down her nose and looked at me. 'My, my,' she said, 'but your breasts have been and gone.' I did not ask her what she meant. And when I swim, she says that my father was never in favour of swimming. He always discouraged it among his men. His men? I asked her if he was in the army and she said of course he wasn't; what put that into my mind?

My mother also has views on the North. 'Dreadful

situation, dreadful, never should have let it happen.' She seems to have read something about Irish history or the North which she keeps talking about. 'You know, I read that the RCs have been treated dreadfully up there. Dreadful time. You see they couldn't vote.' And then she would go back to her book.

I am not allowed to spend money. This, she says, is her last fling. In future she will be too old to go anywhere, and too broke. The money's all gone, she keeps telling me. Then she looks up: 'Have you ever sold any of those paintings, my dear?' I tell her I have but she is already engrossed in her reading.

*

She's living on the proceeds of a house she sold. After that there's her house in London which she's going to sell so that she can move into a maisonette for the aged – at least that's what she calls it.

I feel like a paid companion, not allowed to stray for a single moment. This is why she chose here rather than Venice, I gather. In Venice I would have an excuse to go and look at the pictures and she wouldn't be able to come. Also, Venice has frail, senile old ladies in every nook and cranny. Here at the Hotel Eva, Mother is a novelty. She likes being a novelty.

I feel that at any moment the act will break down and she will be serious as she used to be. This is the woman who ran away when I was little because of what she referred to the other day as her dread fear of the Irish. This is the woman who financed my own escape and has financed my life over the last twenty years, who asked no question but relished each morsel of information I ever gave her about what I was doing with my life. She loves it when I talk of Pallosa. She loves hearing about the festivals, the times we had with Miguel, she loves when I talk in Spanish to the ferryman.

She wants me to go home. It comes a few times a day, a question, a hint. Where is Tom buried? she wanted to know. I didn't know. What did he die of? Then she forgets his name and refers to that man you married when you were young. Once I reminded her of his name she turned and looked at me: 'I think you were right to get away from that hole, my dear.'

She talks about the great-granddaughter in Ireland she has never seen. She would like to leave her something. 'Something valuable, something she would appreciate.' Was she a nice girl? I told her I have not seen Richard since he was a ten-year-old boy so why on earth should I know anything about his daughter. 'Would you mind if I left her my jewellery? You could take a few pieces, but most of it should go to her. Some pieces cost the earth, you know, even in my day. It was what men gave women when they wanted to show their appreciation. Does that boy from the town give you jewels?'

I should never have agreed to come. She is oppressive. I am used to spending so much time alone. Sometimes I lie down on a towel on the beach far enough away from her to pretend I can't hear but she starts to shout at me. I pretend I'm asleep. The other morning she closed her book and said, 'It's funny doing things for the last time. This morning when I was shaving I thought . . .' 'What?' I asked. 'No, little one, I was just making sure you were listening.' I have to face five more weeks of this.

I know she wants me to go back home. What age is Richard now? she asked. I thought for a while. I told her I thought he was almost thirty. And what age is the little girl? I told her I wasn't sure. Two or three. And how long has Tom been dead? I told her five years. And did I ever think of the house? I told her that I did sometimes. Did I like the house? Yes. Did I own the house? Yes, I thought I did. Did I own the farm? I told her that I believed she and I both had a share in the farm. She told me she had a share in nothing. She had left fifty years ago, never looked back and owned nothing. The house was big, wasn't it? She remembered from pictures that the house my father built was big. You could easily get a little flat there, it would be a nice little home for you. Richard wouldn't mind and, after all, you own the house. I told her I wasn't sure I owned the house.

You must go back home. She became emphatic. I listened to her because I thought she was being serious. I told her I was going to stay in Dublin for the moment. For the moment, for the moment, she said it several times. You have no money and you must find a home. Make Richard find you a home. The long, bony fingers of her hand grasped the chair. I suppose the boy from the town has no money. I did not reply. Are you going to marry him? she asked and repeated the question several times. I did not answer her. You must go home, if only to see. She went back to her book and I went into the water and stayed there for as long as I could.

At night from the window we can look down at the

townspeople having their stroll. There is a café just on the waterside where they sit to look at the passers-by. Even at night there's a haze of heat over everything. I am reading *The Ambassadors*, which my mother has just finished. She is asleep now, sound asleep, and will not wake until morning. I am like Chad, still starry-eyed at the sight of the new. I am like Chad who wants the opportunity to see more, to do more. I do not want everything to be over with me. There is more. There is more.

Michael, we have to be good and generous to each other. I will write again when there is more to say. You know I wish you were here. I wish we were all here.

All my love to you,

    Katherine

Home

I will be wearing a grey suit and the first thing you notice about me will be my eyes which tend to fix on things and stare at them. My hair is grey.

Maybe that part of the letter had been too strident; she must be gentler, her son would be nervous of her. It was a cold afternoon in late October: she kept her tweed coat wrapped around her knees. The ticket collector came and punched her ticket.

'Will we arrive in Enniscorthy on time?'

'We'll be a few minutes late, ma'am.'

'It's cold, isn't it?'

'Yes, it is, ma'am.'

After Wicklow the journey did not interest her. She could no longer watch the steely light on the sea. There were fields, a few ugly towns and a sense of order in the countryside, a sense of well-tilled soil. She did not open the book that Michael Graves had given her to read: there was too much to think about.

What did she want? Money, that much was certain. Quite a lot of money, every week, every month, every year, however it suited them. She owned at least three or four hundred acres of the farm. It would be easier if they

185

offered – easier for them and easier for her. She had not mentioned money in the letter. Nor had she told them that she had been living in Dublin for almost six years. In her first letter she had introduced herself, announced that she was in Ireland and said that she would like to see Richard. In her second she had accepted Richard's invitation to come and stay.

What else did she want? She wanted to take a look at her son, once, maybe more. She knew nothing of his wife, nothing, not even a name. And then there was Richard's daughter. But more than anything, she wanted to take stock of the place. She wanted to be there for a while, in the house her father built near the river, some miles from the town.

Outside Gorey the train pulled up and was delayed for some time. She imagined Tom at the station, too fastidious to ask if the train was going to be late. She imagined her son standing there exactly where his father would have stood with the same reserved, distant air. Ungainly. She hoped Richard had left his wife and child at home.

When the train jolted and began to move slowly towards Enniscorthy she realised how much she dreaded what was in store, as though she were in a waiting room with the promise of certain pain. She thought about Richard, and what he would be like. She didn't even know where Tom was buried. She did not know Tom had died until she received a sanctimonious letter from the local clergyman about the good life Tom had led and how he had gone to a better one.

Her train ticket allowed her four days in Enniscorthy;

she had packed clothes for four days. She would not raise the matter of money this time. It was not urgent. This time she would simply be a visitor. She would try and make herself agreeable. In the suitcase she had a teddy bear for her granddaughter.

When she saw the river she knew that they were only minutes away from Enniscorthy. She closed her eyes in dread. She should not have done this. It was a mistake. She should have met him in Dublin first. It was asking too much from both of them.

*

The ticket collector took her case from the rack and put it out on the platform. She had seen Richard from the window as the train stopped. He was much darker and younger-looking than she had imagined. He did not come towards her but stood waiting, looking at her. She waved and he smiled hesitantly. As soon as she lifted the small suitcase he moved towards her. He shook hands with her and led her out into the square where the car was.

'What sort of car do you have? I wondered about that.'

'It's an old Opel. Deirdre's using the other one.'

'Deirdre,' she interrupted. 'That's your wife.'

'Did I not mention her name in my letter?' he asked. 'What's your little girl called?'

'Clare,' he said. 'Clare Proctor. It goes well.'

He started the car in the Railway Square and nosed around slowly towards the bottom of the Shannon.

'It all looks really different,' she said. 'I know that's an obvious thing to say, but there's something missing.'

'There was a fire here, the whole place went up,' he said.

'When? I don't remember it.'

'No,' he said. 'You wouldn't, but it was a big fire. There was a lot of damage done.'

As they crossed the bridge she saw the castle up above them and the two spires of the Protestant and Catholic churches. As he turned towards the Dublin road, she stopped him.

'Can you stop? Can we go somewhere first?' she asked.

'What do you mean, go somewhere?' He seemed disturbed.

'I mean have coffee and talk for a few minutes, or have a drink.'

'We have something ready for you at home.'

'No, I mean just for a few minutes. Could we go back to Bennett's Hotel?'

'Is that what you'd like?'

'You wouldn't mind turning back?'

'Not at all. I'll just stop here for some petrol first.'

He parked the car at the back of the hotel and they went in.

'I'll have a gin and tonic,' she said.

When he sat down he looked at her as though he had a speech prepared.

'I'm sorry if I appeared dramatic. I just didn't want to drive straight there,' Katherine said.

'I don't know whether I should ask you questions or not,' he said and then looked down. She had not thought that he would be shy.

'I don't know either. But I'll start. Where is your wife from?'

'Oh, she's from the town.'

'Here? Enniscorthy, you mean. What's her name?'

'Murphy,' he said.

'Is she one of the Murphys . . .?'

'No,' he interrupted her. 'You don't know the family. I suppose I should tell you that she's R.C.'

'Oh, is she? I hadn't thought of that. I'm such a fool,' she stopped for a minute. 'So you married a girl from the town, an R.C,' she laughed.

'Please don't laugh,' he said.

'No, I'm not laughing at you, Richard. I promise I'm not laughing at you.' He remained silent for a while.

'What should I call you?'

'Well, I call my mother Mother even though she left home when I was about six. She is not well, by the way.'

'I know.'

'I didn't think I told you.'

'No, we've been in correspondence with her.'

'My mother wrote to you?'

'Yes, we've had several long letters. She wrote about London and quite a lot about you.'

'My mother tells lies, you know that?' she said suddenly.

'That's hardly fair,' he said.

'I wish she hadn't written to you about me.'

While they had been talking she had noticed that they were being carefully observed by a man who was sitting at the bar. After a time he approached them and shook her hand.

'You're very welcome home. I'm delighted to see you,' he smiled at her. He had a glass in his hand.

'Can I buy you a drink?' he asked.

'No,' she said. 'We're just going.'

'Just have one,' he said.

'No, we won't, thank you. We're just going,' she said.

'The young man will have one,' the man persisted.

'No, really, thank you. I'm driving,' Richard said.

'But you've just had one. Another one won't bother you.'

'Really, we were just having a conversation and we're going now,' Katherine said.

'Well it's great to see you anyway. I'd say that you'll notice a few changes around Enniscorthy. And many of them for the good.' He stood back for a moment as though he was going to go. 'Well, you're looking well now. Will you be staying long?'

'No, we're going just now,' she said.

'I mean will you be staying long in the area?'

'We must be going now,' she said and stood up. 'See you again.'

The man went back to the bar and put his drink down. He watched them as they walked out. She had no idea who he was.

'I wonder if my mother has written to him as well,' Katherine said as they went across the bridge.

'He's harmless, don't worry about him.'

'What did my mother tell you?'

'That you were in love with a man in Spain and he died.'

'What else?'

'That you had a daughter in Spain.' He stopped. 'Look, it's not fair to ask me what she said.'

'Tell me what else she said.'

'That you have no money.'

'Stop the car.'

They were beyond Blackstoops and nearing Scarawalsh. He paid no attention to her.

'Richard, stop the car.'

'Look, this is my fault. I shouldn't have told you any of this. You see, I didn't know anything about you.'

'Did she write to you before I did?'

'Yes.'

'So you expected my letter?'

'Sort of.'

'What else did she tell you?'

'She told me that the man in Spain killed himself.'

'That's not true. It's a lie.'

The river was now in view. It was full and muddy.

'She should not have written to you.'

'I wrote to her first,' he said.

'You wrote to her?'

He stopped the car and turned off the engine.

'Yes. I didn't know if she was still alive, but I had an address and I wrote to her just after Christmas. She wrote back and then I asked her to let me know about you, about where you were and what you were doing. You see Clare was learning to talk and she asked because she sees a lot of Deirdre's parents. I told her my father was dead and she understood that but when I told her my mother was in Spain she was fascinated. She talked about you all the time. You see, I thought you might never contact us ever and I wanted to make some connection, I wanted to know something. When my father died I could not contact you.'

'Did she tell you anything else?'

'Well, there were a lot of things. She said you had a friend, a man.'

'Did she tell you his name?'

'Yes, she said he was from the town. She said he was RC.'

'So you know all about me.'

'Deirdre recognised his name, your friend, some of his family still live in the town.'

He started the car again. It was now almost dark. He switched the headlights on.

'I want to talk to you soon about my leaving. I don't want it to be something we can't talk about. I mean my leaving you all those years ago and not coming back until now.'

'I should like to know about it,' he said.

'Did my mother not tell you why I left?'

'She said you hated Ireland.'

'That's rubbish. She is the one who hates Ireland – or thinks she does. I have never hated Ireland.'

'Did you hate my father?'

'No, I certainly didn't hate your father.'

When they reached Clohamon he crossed the bridge.

'Why are we going the long way around?' she asked.

'Because we want to talk.'

'I am really upset about my mother giving such a false picture of me.'

He did not reply.

'What is Deirdre like?' she asked.

'How can I answer? She's nice.'

'Does she mind my arriving suddenly like this?'

'She's a bit puzzled I suppose. She certainly doesn't mind.'

'Does she like the house?'

'Yes, yes, she does.'

'Has she made many changes?'

'Yes, she has. She's done a lot. The house had become a bit shabby with just two men living in it for so long.'

'Were you lonely there?'

'No, it was all right.'

'Did your father ever talk about me after I left?' she asked.

'He did for a while. He said you'd gone away and you'd be back, but then he went to Dublin one day and came home and told me that you'd not be back, that you had left, and that was that. I don't think your name came up again. We both thought about you, of course. And I saw your name in the paper once to do with an art show in Dublin, but my father would not pay any attention when I showed it to him.' He looked at her. 'We're nearly there. Is it okay if we just go straight in? They'll be expecting us.'

'Let's go in.'

*

'Come in the back way,' Richard said as he took her case from the car. His wife and daughter were at the kitchen table. The size of the kitchen shocked her, and she stood back for a moment, until the little girl came running

193

towards her. 'I did a drawing for you. Look, I did a drawing for you.' Then her daughter-in-law came towards her and kissed her on the cheek.

'I'm very pleased to meet you,' she said.

Katherine looked about the room. The range was still where it had been, but the room was twice the size. As she spoke to Deirdre she realised that the dividing wall between the kitchen and the pantry had been knocked down.

Deirdre was tall and thin and her hair was cut closely around her face. Her eyes were blue and her mouth was small.

'Maybe you'd like to go upstairs,' she said to Katherine.

'Yes, maybe Clare will show me where to go.' The child had been sitting staring at her grandmother. 'I have a present for you.'

'Yes, Clare, you know where your grandmother is sleeping, don't you? Why don't you take her up there now?'

There were fitted carpets everywhere, all the old rugs were gone. The walls of the hall and the stairs were painted crimson, hung with pictures of foxes and hounds. She would not have recognised the house: a considerable amount of money had been spent on redecoration and, she felt, it had been done with a certain taste.

'We thought you might be used to continental food,' Deirdre said when she came down, 'so I have been practising my lasagne all week.' There was a bottle of red wine on the table and a salad. 'Your mother said you had a great time in Portugal in the summer. We could all do with a holiday like that.'

Katherine smiled. 'Yes, everybody made a great fuss of her. She enjoys that. But she's not well at the moment.'

After dinner they went into the sitting room. Clare kissed everybody goodnight and went to bed. They opened another bottle of wine and talked for a while, about Dublin, the weather, Enniscorthy, neighbours. The room was painted yellow. Huge plants in tubs all over made it look smaller. The best of the old rugs were on the floor which had been sanded and varnished. There was a colour television in the corner of the room. It took Katherine a while to realise that there were radiators in the room as well as the fire. A lot of the furniture in the room was made of cane. She had the feeling that the room had been decorated with the help of a book or a glossy woman's magazine.

She lay in bed that night for a long time before she turned off the light. It was hard to believe that Michael Graves had seen her off on the train at only one o'clock that day.

*

She had not drawn the curtains. She woke to a flood of light. She put on the dressing-gown hanging on the back of the door and sat by the window. The house was as solid and splendid as ever. Her father used to say that he was glad when the old house burnt down – he was then able to build the house he always wanted. Her bedroom window looked out over the lawn which stretched to the river. The boathouse was still there. Perhaps it would be a good day to take out a boat and row for a while. She was restless, it was like being in a familiar hotel –

eventually she would have to brave the staircase and be nice to someone.

Her first visitor was Clare, still in her nightdress and carrying her new teddy bear.

'Mummy says I can call him Rupert if I want to.'

'That's all right with me, although I thought you might call him Pedro.'

'I want to call him Rupert.'

'Then call him Rupert. We'll all call him Rupert. You'd better decide because he will only answer to one name.'

'Bears can't talk.'

'No, but they can understand.'

'You're silly.'

'You're silly.'

'Mummy wants to know if you want tea or coffee.'

'Tell her I'm getting dressed and I'll be down.'

'Why are you getting dressed?'

'Because it's time to get dressed. Are you going to come out for a walk with me today?'

'Can Rupert come?'

*

'I must compliment you on what you've done to the kitchen,' she said to Deirdre.

'I thought it needed a bit of modernising all right.' Deirdre looked away as she spoke. Katherine thought that she was nervous.

'Do you cook much?'

'Oh I do yes,' Deirdre said. 'I was going to send you up your breakfast.'

'I'm much happier having my breakfast down here. Have you had yours?'

'I had mine with Richard before he went out. We're thinking of going off early. Did he ask if it was all right with you?'

'No, he didn't say anything,' Katherine replied.

'We booked seats for a concert in Wexford, you know, the festival is on. We were going to go to an opera but we thought you'd prefer to see Wexford in the afternoon, and maybe do a bit of shopping.'

Nothing was further from Katherine's mind than shopping, but if they wanted her to go she would. On this October day all she wanted to do was walk by the river or across the fields until the light faded.

'Maybe you don't want to? We could cancel the tickets. I don't know what concert it is, but Richard does – it's part of the festival.'

'No, I'd love to go. I'd love to go to Wexford.'

After her breakfast Katherine went to the hall to fetch her coat, and walked out alone, down the drive to the road. It had rained during the night and the grass was soaking. There were new fences up. The house had been repainted a different shade of yellow. She was glad it was still yellow. That had always been part of her father's plan. A big, solid, yellow house by the river. There was a white light coming in from between the trees and she could watch the October sun between the clouds. The ditches on either side of the road were still overgrown with weeds and ferns and grass. This damp growth, these small roads unfolding into the countryside with trees and ditches on either side. Larch, beech, oak, ash, chestnut, birch. It was just as she had remembered: the sogginess, the constant rain, the soaking grass.

She turned off the road and went down a lane leading to the river. She was wearing the wrong shoes and they soon became wet and muddy. The river was flowing fast and full. New trees had been planted opposite where the fields sloped up to the Bunclody road. Down-river she could see the yellow house standing in the open meadow and the huge beech trees beside it. The sky darkened – the green of the grass, the river and the trees changed too, darkened. She walked as fast as she could through the wet grass by the side of the river to avoid the rain. Just as she scaled the fence to enter the grounds of the house proper the rain came. She could hear it bounce against the river and then hit the grass, then it reached her. She ran back to the house and found Deirdre in the kitchen.

'We're nearly ready to go to Wexford. We were going to have lunch in the Talbot. Richard wondered if you might prefer to stay here,' Deirdre said.

'No, no,' Katherine replied, 'I do want to go. Can you wait just for a while?'

*

They insisted Katherine sit in the front seat. They had left Clare with the housekeeper. They drove by the river as far as Edermine and then along the cement road to Oylgate. They were silent apart from a few comments on the weather – it had stopped raining. They reached Ferrycarrig.

'Have you ever thought of coming down here to paint?' Deirdre asked her.

'No, it's a bit too pretty for me really. I've never done beauty spots, round towers, that sort of thing.'

They were driving into Wexford.

'This is the only town in Ireland I actually like,' Katherine said.

'Don't you like Enniscorthy?' Deirdre asked.

'I suppose that too and for the same reasons as Wexford, the stone buildings and the narrow streets, but Enniscorthy doesn't have the sea like Wexford although I suppose it has hills to make up for it. Still, I think I prefer Wexford. I love all that water.'

Richard parked in the car park opposite the Talbot Hotel and they went in for lunch.

'What is the concert?' Katherine asked him.

'A quartet,' he said. 'I read in the *Irish Times* it's meant to be a very good one. I think it's Beethoven.'

'Richard says you like music,' Deirdre said.

'Yes,' Katherine replied.

They walked up to the Main Street.

'It's very busy of course. Friday's the big shopping day,' Deirdre said. Katherine nodded. The Main Street was indeed crowded, the shops all had special offers for the Opera Festival.

'Do you enjoy opera?' Deirdre asked.

'Yes,' Katherine said. 'Do you?'

'I find it a bit heavy,' Deirdre said.

They turned off the Main Street and walked up the hill towards the Theatre Royal. There was a crowd at the door when they arrived.

'Quite a few people here are from Enniscorthy,' Deirdre said. 'They must be down for the day, like us.'

As they walked in, Deirdre began to greet people in the foyer. She then led two women over to Katherine and Richard. 'This is my mother-in-law.' Both women looked at Katherine who shook hands and nodded.

'It must be great to be home,' one of the women said and they both looked at her intently to see what she would say.

'Yes, lovely, thank you,' Katherine said.

'Let's go in,' she turned to Richard. Deirdre was still talking to the two women.

'Let's just wait a minute,' he said.

'Do you know these quartets?' she asked him.

'I'm afraid I don't have much time for music.'

'I thought you were a gentleman farmer.'

'I am a gentleman who is out of my bed at seven o'clock every morning.'

'What sort of farming are you doing now?'

'We still have a good dairy herd and we do a bit of tillage.'

'I went for a walk this morning and I didn't see any cows.'

'They're in the fields around the house but you wouldn't have seen them this morning.'

'When I ran the farm they were everywhere,' she said. She smiled at him. They took their seats.

Deirdre came in and sat beside Katherine.

'There's a whole gang of them down from Enniscorthy.' She looked around the Theatre Royal. 'God, it's small, isn't it? How many would this place hold?'

'I don't know,' Katherine said, 'two or three hundred?'

The lights went down and the quartet came on. The first piece was bright and airy. The quartet seemed good-humoured playing it. It was easy in the small theatre to concentrate on the music. The second quartet was more sombre, the violins returning again and again to a series of shivering notes.

'Do you not find it a bit dull?' Deirdre asked Katherine at the interval.

'No, I'm enjoying it immensely. What do you think of it, Richard?' Katherine turned to her son.

'I wish I could do this every Saturday afternoon.' Richard smiled.

'Well, I just wondered,' Deirdre said, 'if you were bored, maybe we could go and look around the shops.'

'Let's go out in the air for a moment anyway,' Richard said.

They went into the foyer.

'Do you like Dublin?' Deirdre asked.

'The city itself – no. But I like the area I live in. It suits me for the moment.'

'I love going up to Dublin for the day,' Deirdre said.

Katherine wished she would stop talking.

Richard lit a cigarette and stood at the door. He stood there until a bell sounded for the second half of the concert.

'I think I'll slip off now and do a bit of shopping, does anyone mind?' Deirdre said. 'I'll meet you back in the Talbot. Or what about White's?'

Richard said they would meet her in White's.

Katherine and Richard went back to their seats in

silence. The third quartet was sadder, jerkier, more complex. She could sense that Richard responded to the music. His father had never been interested in classical music; listening to the music, she regretted she had not contacted Richard when Tom died. She put her head down and her hands over her face.

A slow movement began. She looked up at the four players, the lighted stage. The music was intense and purposeful. For one moment when she changed position her hand brushed Richard's. He caught her hand and held it. She looked at him but the expression on his face did not change. He continued to listen to the music. He held her hand until the slow movement ended.

*

The following day Katherine walked about Enniscorthy while Deirdre shopped. In ways Enniscorthy reminded her of a Catalan town, Llavorsi, maybe, or Poble de Segur, all hills with a river flowing through. And the cold too reminded her of there, the crisp, bracing cold. She crossed the bridge and walked down by the river. There were no boats now on the river, the cotmen who were there when she was young had long disappeared, but there were still warehouses at the bottom of the Abbey Square. She tried to find the old coffee house on the Turret Rocks above the town but it seemed to have gone.

All the things she remembered. How still and unchanged it was. How the road out from Doherty's Garage to the graveyard was overhung with trees. The stones on the bridge at Scarawalsh. The ruined Tower on Vinegar Hill. How the lights came on in the shops at half four or five in November, and there was a sense of busy warmth in the Market Square in Enniscorthy. The steps that went up the bare rock behind Bennett's Hotel.

After dinner back at the house she fell asleep by the fire to be woken by the television which Richard turned on. She went to her room and tried to make out the river as it flowed past. It was very tiring being home.

The next morning she could find nobody when she searched the house. Finally, she found the housekeeper in the kitchen. 'Where are Deirdre and Clare?'

'Ah, they've gone to mass in the town, ma'am,' the woman said. 'They went in the car with Mr Proctor.'

'Richard has gone too?'

'Yes, ma'am, he's gone in to mass in the town as well.'

'You mean he's gone into service.'

'No, ma'am, he's gone into mass. They always go to mass together, the three of them,' the woman said.

'I see,' Katherine said, 'thank you.'

She returned upstairs. Richard went to mass, this was news; no one had told her. She should not have left Richard on his own when Tom died; she should have come back sooner than this. She was surprised at how upset she was about him going to mass; she did not know she had prejudices left like that. Had he left the Church of Ireland altogether?

She went back down to the kitchen and waited for them to return. She noticed the prayer book in Deirdre's hand when she came in the door. The child also had a prayer book but Richard had none.

'My parents are coming for Sunday dinner. They are looking forward to meeting you,' Deirdre said.

203

Katherine waited until Richard left the room to go upstairs and she followed him to his bedroom.

'I didn't know that you had become an RC,' she said to Richard as he stood beside the door.

'Yes, I should have told you.'

'Why?' she said, 'why did you do it?' She knew she sounded irritated.

'I don't want to talk about it now,' he said.

'Why not?'

'You seem hostile.'

'I'm not hostile, I'm puzzled,' she said, 'or maybe I am hostile.'

He sighed.

'Also, do you mind if I don't have dinner. Deirdre says her parents are coming and I just don't feel up to meeting them. I just couldn't bear it – all that talking. They seem to chatter on about nothing.'

'You've never met her parents.'

'I hope you don't mind if I don't sit with you for dinner, that's all I have to say.'

He was staring at something behind her and she knew as she turned that it was Deirdre.

'Aren't you feeling well?' Deirdre asked.

'I'm just not up to meeting people. I'm sorry,' Katherine said.

'Would you like dinner in your room?' Deirdre asked.

'Yes, I would if it's not any trouble.'

'It's just that my parents were looking forward to meeting you.'

'Tell them I'm really very sorry.'

*

She would leave first thing in the morning and she would not come back. Money was still a problem but it would have to be sorted out some other way. She would not come back. This would be her last day in this room. It was pouring outside. The housekeeper brought in a tray of roast beef, vegetables and a glass of wine.

The sky brightened in the early afternoon. Katherine wondered if she could creep out of the house without anybody noticing. She put on a raincoat she found in the wardrobe and some wellingtons which Deirdre had given her and went down the stairs. No sound. As she reached the front door she heard a voice behind a door on the right. She fled into the porch and closed the door behind her.

She walked around towards the back of the house, and then to the river. The rain had almost stopped, yet there were still heavy clouds in the sky. She paused to listen: a slight murmur of water. It was strange how flat the banks of the river were, and yet how it never seemed to over-flow. She walked up along the river as far as she could. The rain held out as she retraced her steps and watched the evening falling in over the fields, the darkness coming in from Mount Leinster; she tried to keep everything else out of her mind and concentrate on what she could see.

As she approached the house she could make out a few figures standing around in front of the porch; they were waiting for her and had seen her. She moved in their direction and saw it was Richard, Deirdre and Clare, with two other people who she presumed were Deirdre's parents.

'How do you do? I'm Deirdre's mother. I've heard all about you. We're really pleased to meet you.' The woman smiled at Katherine. 'This is my husband,' she continued, pointing at the man who had gone over to the car. 'We're sorry you weren't feeling well. I was going to hop up and make sure you were all right but Deirdre said maybe it would be better to leave you alone, didn't you Dee?' She looked at her daughter. 'Isn't it great the way the weather has kept up?' she said. 'Did you have a nice walk? We were going to go for a walk ourselves but we thought it was a bit wet. Maybe you'll get used to it now and stay for a while. Isn't it nice down here?'

'I'm going back tomorrow, actually.' Katherine looked at Richard but his head was bent down.

'Isn't it a nice house all the same?' the woman continued. 'We often used to look at it from the road when we'd be out for a drive and we'd admire it and there we were today having our dinner in it. Isn't it great the way things change?'

'It is indeed,' Katherine said. 'I'd really better go inside and change these wellingtons. Delighted to meet you both.'

She was sitting in an armchair by the bedroom window when Clare came to the door.

'Are you really my granny from Spain?'

'Yes, I am.'

'You're much younger than my other granny.'

'Yes that's true,' Katherine said, 'some grannies can be younger than others.'

'And you know my great-granny in London, is she your mummy?'

'Yes, she is.'

'We're going to see her in London.'

'Are you?'

Deirdre came into the room.

'I was looking for Clare. Come with me now, Clare, you're not to be disturbing your grandmother.'

'She's not disturbing me,' Katherine said.

'It's her bedtime anyway.'

Richard was reading one of the Sunday papers. Several lamps were alight in the sitting-room and a log fire was burning in the grate.

'How comfortable this house has become,' Katherine said. 'You live very well now, don't you? Tell me, do you love Deirdre?'

He looked up and faced her for a moment. 'It's not a question I want to answer. But yes, yes I do. And I don't want any trouble about that, I really don't.'

'Do you think I would make trouble?'

'I don't know you.'

'Do they come here often, her parents?'

'I'm not going to talk about them.'

'They seem very friendly anyhow,' Katherine said.

'Yes, they're very nice.'

'The mother talks non-stop, doesn't she?'

Richard folded his newspaper.

'Could you get me a drink?' Katherine asked him.

'What would you like?'

'Anything.'

'What?'

'A gin and tonic?'

He went out to the kitchen and came back with her drink. Deirdre came downstairs after putting Clare to bed.

'Deirdre,' Richard said, 'would you mind if we talk on our own for a while.' Deirdre went out. He stood with his elbow on the mantelpiece first but then sighed and sat down opposite Katherine.

'What do you want to say to me?' she asked.

'This. You are going to be in Ireland for a while. You are short of money. No, don't interrupt me, your mother tells me you are short of money. You are unhappy in some ways and we want to see something of you, and to help you if we can. There's one thing you need to know for this to happen. You might have guessed but I'm telling you anyway. Until I was ten years old I lived with two people who hardly spoke to each other or to anyone else, and who had no friends. From the time I was ten until I was thirteen and after that during the holidays, I had a father who hardly spoke and who had no friends. When I came back here to the farm it was to night after night of silence, of isolation. My father died from isolation and loneliness and I didn't enjoy watching that. And I don't like the cold rooms I was brought up in. I hate everything about the way I was brought up. I like this house now, I like my wife, my daughter, and my wife's family. Will you please not sneer at them?' He looked at her directly. He seemed close to tears.

'I don't know if you remember what happened here. When the house was burned to the ground. These people, the locals . . .'

He stopped her. 'I remember other things that happened here,' he said. 'You abandoned me. I remember how I felt then. So how dare you talk about my relations like that? You have no right. The people who burnt this house down are long dead.'

'I'm going anyway in the morning,' she said. 'What time is the train?'

'I don't know,' he said and went over to the television to turn it on.

'Could you find out for me?' she raised her voice.

'It goes at twenty past eight,' he said and came back to sit down. 'I'll drive you there.'

'Good. You can wake me in the morning. I'll have my things ready.'

'Will you not sit with us for a while?'

'And do what?' she said.

'And talk, perhaps,' he said and laughed to himself.

'I'm going to bed, Richard. I'll see you in the morning.'

*

In the morning, she woke to a grey light as the dawn came. She dressed and walked down to the river to look at the early morning mist over the Slaney. It was as she had always remembered. When she went back into the house by the kitchen Richard was there.

'Sorry,' she said. 'I didn't mean to frighten you.'

'I thought you were a ghost,' he said.

'I am. That's what I am, a ghost.'

'I was going to make breakfast before I woke you.'

'You must tell Deirdre I am sorry,' she said.

'I shall, I'll tell her that.'

'I will write to her, maybe I will suggest we meet in Dublin.'

'I'm sure she'd love to meet you in Dublin.'

'Tell her that, will you?'

'I shall. I promise I'll tell her that.'

'And I'll think about what you said to me.'

'I'm sorry, I shouldn't have said it.'

'No, Richard. I'm pleased that you did. How little one considers other people.'

He drove her towards the town by the back road. There was no traffic.

'How wonderful it all is,' she said. 'The hanging trees.'

'Are you glad you came?'

'Yes I am. I'm sorry. It's so difficult.'

They drove along the Rectory Road and turned down to the station.

'We're early,' he said. 'We'll wait in the car.'

'No, no. Please, leave me here. I want to be on my own,' she insisted and made as though to get out.

'Well, I'll go in with you for a second.'

They walked into the station where a few people were already waiting.

'I must talk to you about money,' he said.

'Another time,' she replied.

'Why not now?'

'Because we don't know one another well enough. The next time we meet we'll talk about it.'

'I have some to give you now.'

'Don't give me any now.'

'When will we see you again?'

'I will write. You go now and I'll see you soon. Give my love to Deirdre and Clare.'

★

He left her there in the grey morning to watch the manse up on the hill; he now paid his dues to the priests who lived there. If Katherine's father had ever imagined such a thing! Cold grey light of the morning in Enniscorthy, the Slaney running softly towards Wexford and the sea, the Dublin train moving past the river and the Ringwood and Davis's Mills and then under the tunnel at the Model School to cross the bridge and arrive at the station where she was waiting.

The Sea

The sea. A grey shine on the sea. Every morning Michael
Graves left Katherine and walked into Blackwater to buy
whatever food they needed and a newspaper. Katherine
had not painted in a long while. Sometimes Michael's
comments irritated her but she paid no attention. Sea,
sky, land. Connections. The port of Barcelona; the sea at
Sitges in the bright grey early morning; the mud flats
at Faro on a brilliant day, all shimmer and glare. And
then this, this too. The dull grey light on the gun-metal
sea at Ballyconnigar. Each colour a subtle variation of
another: cream, silver, light blue, light green, dark grey.

Michael built her a windshield. Nothing was firm in
this light. At first she worked in water colours on small
sheets of paper, using a crayon to make the lines. It was
hard to paint how the waves separated from the sky, it
was difficult not to give it too much definition.

'All my summers were spent in a hut when I was
young.' Michael showed her the tiny wooden hut which
his father had rented. 'It was this spot here, this exact
spot,' he pointed at the ground and made her look. 'On
the first Sunday in the summer of 1947 I knew I was for
it. I knew for certain I was done for.' He searched her

eyes again to make sure that she understood. 'I spent two years in the sanitorium. I was lucky I didn't die. The best of them died. Three or four in a family died.'

That summer Michael talked a lot about the past in Enniscorthy. Lives she knew nothing of, although she lived so few miles away: the poverty, the despair, the emigration. Some afternoons Michael met friends from his schooldays in Blackwater and did not return until the early hours of the morning. There was only one room in the hut and the bed was small; she disliked the smell of alcohol when he came in late, but otherwise she was happy to get on with her work and leave him to Blackwater and his friends.

She asked him to help her stretch a canvas, so big that she would have to leave it outside at night covered by plastic. He told her it was too ambitious, he told her to go easy, but she insisted. She would start with the grey Wexford light on a grey July day, with a certain pale yellow warmth. And work from memory with the canvas leaning against the side of the hut. She would make everything fade into itself, build the colours up carefully so there was a texture: the sea a vague shimmer of grey light.

He would get up in the early afternoon and come out with his shirt unbuttoned and look at what she was doing. He would tell her over and over that she was working on too large a scale. One day she turned to him and said: 'Can we rent this place for another month?' He was going into the village and said he would try to arrange it.

'Can you watch one hour with me?' He grinned at

her. He stood as though waiting for her. 'I have no money,' he continued suddenly.

'I thought you had the gallery money,' she said.

'I spent it.'

'Don't worry. I think I can give you some. But will you promise me something? Will you please?'

'What? What do you want me to do?'

'I want you to stop saying I'm working on too large a scale. I know I'm working on too large a scale.'

'So you want me to be the man who just helps to stretch the canvases.' He began to move away.

'Michael, where are you going?'

'I'm going into the village.'

'Do you have to go? What are you going to do there?'

'Ah, I'll meet someone I know.'

'Do you want me to come with you?'

'No.'

'You don't want me to come? Why can't I come?'

At first he didn't answer and she asked again.

'We might meet people,' he said.

'And what's wrong with that?'

'Think for a minute.'

'You don't want them to meet me?'

'They come in with their wives. This is Ireland. It's the country.'

'And I'm not your wife.'

'They all know that you're here and who you are.'

'So why can't we have a drink together?'

'Because they would be uncomfortable. They're ordinary people I grew up with.'

'I think you mean *you* would be uncomfortable.'

She stood with her arms wrapped around her as though she were cold. There was silence between them for some time.

'Do you need some money?' she asked.

'Aye, Missus,' he said.

'I'm in need of a few drinks myself, but since you won't let me drink with your friends I'll go on my own.'

'Go where?'

'Into the village.'

'When?'

'Whenever I feel like it, later on.'

'Come now then,' he said.

'Why don't we walk to Curracloe,' she said. 'I'll have a swim on the way.'

'It's too cold for bathing,' he said.

'We can have our tea in the hotel.'

'It's a long walk.'

'It's even longer when you're sober,' she said.

'Why won't you come to Blackwater?' he asked.

'You don't want me to come.'

'We can go to Mrs Davis's, there's never anybody there.'

'Michael has the landlord's daughter but he keeps her in the hut,' she began to sing as though it were a rhyme. He looked at her and laughed.

'Let's go to Curracloe,' he said.

She put her swimsuit and towel into a string carrier bag and asked him to help her cover the canvas with plastic before they went. Although it was still early afternoon a grey haze had come down over the sea and the fog horn was blaring.

'Tuskar lighthouse will start soon and go until

morning,' he said. 'The weather is going to get fine. There's going to be a heatwave.'

'Are you sure?'

'I am, but it'll only last a few days. In 1959 it lasted the whole summer. That summer I painted the hill up there behind the hut again and again and I sold every one of them.'

'You painted here as well?'

'As well as what?'

'As well as me?'

'They were as good anyway.'

'I never knew that you painted here,' she tried to keep him serious.

'I remember this first when the coast was out nearly another half mile. It gets eaten away every winter, that hill above Keating's used to have a watchtower. It was a great hill to sit with a book.'

'Do you have any family around here?'

'No, not around here. In Enniscorthy. I'd introduce you only you won't marry me.'

'I'm going for a swim,' she said, 'you'll have to come after me if you want to marry me.'

She changed into her bathing costume. Michael sat on the sand with his hands clasped around his knees and stared out to sea. He looked old and despondent. When she waded out she found the water even colder than she expected. She stood for a while shivering in the cold sea.

'Michael, it's freezing,' she shouted back to him.

'Only a Protestant would go for a swim on a day like today.'

'Watch me Michael, watch me. One, two, three.' The

first shock, then pleasure as she lay on her back and kicked hard in the freezing water.

When she came out of the sea he had the towel ready for her.

'Aren't you the brave woman, aren't you?'

'It's lovely when you're in the water. I wish you'd come in with me some day.'

'It's thirty years since I've been in the sea.' They made their way past Flaherty's Gap and Ballyvaloo.

'I could have stayed here all my life,' he said. 'I could have been down here all the time,' he stopped and looked out to sea. They were nearing Ballineskar.

Something had loosened in him; he started to tell her about Brownswood sanitorium, about Enniscorthy, about Ballyconnigar, how when they got older they used to rent a place, a few of them, his brother, friends, fellow teachers. The others came and went but he always stayed the full two months.

'I read everything up there. Dickens, Shakespeare, George Eliot, Herman Melville. I'd go up on the hill and maybe just lie in the sun, and at night we'd sit around and talk or play cards. No one drank then.

'We always used to talk about the last day of summer when we'd have to pack up our stuff and go back to the town. We'd all go for a swim that day and stay in the water as long as we could. The first time I coughed blood I went straight in for a swim. Straight into the sea. I knew I was dying. I'll never forget it. I must have stayed in an hour, thinking this would really be the last day. I tried to concentrate on it so I would never forget it.'

Suddenly, as they got near Curracloe, the flashes from the lighthouse began.

'There used to be another lighthouse,' he said. 'The Blackwater Lightship, which flashed with a fainter light. I used to paint them in the twilight.'

'I'd love to see some of those paintings.'

'I'll never paint down here again.'

He was morose, but she let him go on just as he had often listened to her.

'A few of them used to come on bicycles to visit me in Brownswood sanitorium. They always had such a look of doom as if they were sick and dying instead of me. I'd be upset for a whole day after they left. I used to go off for a walk, sometimes the nurses would let me go up to the top of the hill so I could see the Ringwood and the river. That's how I started painting. I was getting worse that time. So one day, my brother asked me if there was anything I wanted and I said some paints and a bit of board.

'So they all clubbed in, about ten of them, my brother and some of the fellows, and bought me a load of oil paints and brushes and an easel. It was like a farewell present and it was the only time I ever cried. Some in that ward still died even though the streptomycin became available soon afterwards. A lot of them had no faith in the cure.' He sat down and took off his shoes to shake the sand out.

As they walked on up the hill towards the hotel, it started to drizzle. The bar was empty except for one couple with their children. She gave him money to buy her a gin and tonic; he had a pint of Guinness.

'I remember how ill you looked when I met you first in Barcelona. Your skin was all yellow.'

He didn't reply.

'Does being back in Ballyconnigar upset you?' she asked him.

'I don't know. I suppose if you hadn't been here I would never have come back.'

'Are you really sorry you left Ireland?'

'No, I'm not. I was just being sentimental about what it would be like if I hadn't left. I used to hate it. I used to hate facing teaching every morning.' He spoke slowly, as though he found it difficult to find the words.

'How long did you teach?'

'I started in 1940 and I kept at it until I went into the sanitorium.'

'I was married in 1940,' she said.

'In Enniscorthy?'

'No, Tom wanted to go to Ferns Cathedral for some reason I can't remember.'

'Are you ever sorry you left him?'

'No.'

'Are you going to visit your family often?'

'Yes, I am. Richard and Deirdre have said they'll do up one of the outhouses for me. It'll be private, away from them. You'll be able to come and stay. They're building a studio. I'm going to spend a lot of time with them.'

'They must like you.'

'My son likes me.'

'Do you like your son?'

'Yes,' she laughed, 'yes, I didn't think I would, but I do.'

'Is he like you?'

'No, he looks exactly like his father. Even when he was a child he used to look and behave exactly like his father.'

They talked for the rest of the afternoon until it was time for tea; every so often she would find that his mind had wandered – he was thinking again, brooding over the past. He wanted to sit near the window so he could see the lighthouse. Outside the drizzle continued.

'Do you know something?' he said. 'I have always thought the social difference between us was the reason you could not marry me.'

'Social difference?'

She was puzzled by the importance he seemed to be giving this.

'Yes, where you're from and where I'm from.'

'I thought other things were in the way,' she said.

'Like what?' he asked.

'My being with Miguel when I met you. I have never recovered from what happened, you know that. By the way, social considerations don't make any difference to me.'

'I think they make a difference to everything you do and say.'

'They make no difference to my relationship with you.'

'I think they do.'

'How, tell me how.'

'I don't think you would ever marry a Catholic.'

'This is mad. It's just loony talk. Let's go.'

He said he wanted another drink.

'You turn nasty when you drink.'

'I want another drink. And you have the money.'

'If you're drinking, I'm going to drink,' she said.

At closing time Michael asked the barman for a bottle of whiskey and some Guinness. Katherine wanted to try and find a car but it was too late and there were none.

By the time they reached the marsh at the bottom of the hill in Curracloe they were both wet.

'How are we going to find our way along the strand?' Katherine asked as soon as they felt the sand under their feet.

'Tuskar, the light of Tuskar,' Michael replied.

'Why don't we go back and stay in the hotel for the night?'

'The walk to Ballyconnigar will do us good. Come on, the hotel's probably booked out already.'

'It'll take hours.'

'We'll do it in an hour if we walk fast.'

They linked arms and tried to walk fast. Drops of water were dripping down the back of Katherine's neck. A few times they found themselves at the edge of the sea.

'How far have we come?' she asked him.

'I think we should be getting near Ballyvaloo,' he said.

'Is this half way?'

He stood in the drizzle at the edge of the sea and held her against him. His breath sounded as though he were sobbing. She listened. At first she couldn't make out what he said. Then he spoke again. 'Don't leave me destitute, sure you won't?'

She reached for his hand and she held it hard as though she was trying to hurt him.

'No, I won't. I promise I won't.'

They walked on in silence.

'When we wake up,' Michael said, 'it'll be a fine blue day.'

'We're nearly there now, aren't we?' she said.

'Just another bit. It won't take us long.'

The Slaney

It was a Sunday morning in December. Katherine went down the spiral staircase from the low-ceilinged bedroom to the living room below. At the back of the converted outhouse was the studio from where she could see a half mile stretch of the river. Her work of the previous month lay about the studio, resting against the walls.

Despite the studies she had made, and despite her intense concentration day after day, painting from early morning and working long into the evening, despite this exhaustive involvement in the work, she was still unsure, she still felt that some of the work was too abstract.

Between the outhouse and the studio there was an old building where she had stored paintings and sketches going back over thirty years. To relax for an hour or two during the day, she worked on paintings that had been half done over the years in Dublin, in the Pyrenees and in Barcelona. But she knew that eventually she would have to face the present work.

*

She wanted to have a show which was not a collection of scraps, work done in bits and pieces. It was ten years

225

since her previous exhibition. She had shown work from Spain in the Dawson Gallery; she had been included in the Living Art in Dublin; she still had all the Ballyconnigar watercolours and oils. She was ready to exhibit these watercolours and have them framed, but the oils, she believed, would take years to complete.

The Slaney north of Enniscorthy and south of Bunclody. This was the land the English had taken over and tilled. They had cut down the trees, they had given new names to each thing, as though they were the first to live there. In the beginning she had been trying to paint the land as though it had no history, only colours and contours. Had the light changed as the owners changed? How could it matter? At dawn and dusk she walked along by the river. In the morning there was a mist along the Slaney, palpable, grey, lingering. In the evening at four when the light faded, an intense calm descended on the river, a dark blue stillness as though glass were moving from Wicklow to the sea, even the sounds then were muted, a few crows in the trees, cattle in the distance and the faint noise of water.

*

She began to work; she started to paint as though she was trying to catch the landscape rolling backwards into history, as though horizon was a time as well as a place. Dusk on the Slaney. Over and over. Dusk on the Slaney and the sense of all dusks that have come and gone in one spot in one country, the time it was painted to stand for all time, with all time's ambiguities.

In the distance the rebels lie bleeding.

226

In the distance no one has yet set foot.

In the distance a car is moving.

In the distance the sanitorium at Brownswood in Enniscorthy.

In the distance Enniscorthy Castle squats at the top of a hill.

In the distance is the light and the darkness falling, the clouds moving, the Blackstairs Mountains above Bunclody, Mount Leinster, the full moon rising.

*

She often worked at the end of the promenade along the Slaney, near Enniscorthy. She faced down the river. She had planned twenty-four paintings and asked Michael Graves to help her stretch that number of canvases, each the same size: just under six feet in height and four feet in width. She could chart each one, first on paper with crayons and then on a smaller canvas. When the time came to paint on the big scale she did so indoors, under artificial light. She waited until the evening and worked in the studio.

She made it clear to Richard and Deirdre that they were to visit her whenever they wished. Michael Graves had years before told her the story of the man from Porlock who had disturbed Coleridge when the poet was writing Kubla Khan in a frenzy of ecstasy and concentration. It became a joke. Clare became the little girl from Porlock and Richard the man from Porlock. Clare came after school and talked for an hour or two, or went for a walk or drove with her into Enniscorthy. She also did some painting or played in the studio.

Richard visited at lunchtime. Katherine had taken a stereo into the studio but she never listened to music when she was working. She played some music for Richard every day. As soon as he came in she put on a record and made him guess what it was. He adopted the habit of lying on the floor dressed in his work clothes, his eyes closed, not saying anything, listening to the music. If there was a light on in the evening he would come in for half an hour and talk. Deirdre did not come unless she had a message or an excuse.

'You've been so good to me since I came back,' Katherine said to her one day. 'I really appreciate what you've done.'

'It was the least we could do,' Deirdre said.

'No,' Katherine insisted, 'I am talking more about *you*, how much you have done and how good you have been.'

'But I've done nothing,' Deirdre said.

'You have. This whole studio and the outhouse were all your work.'

'Oh I enjoyed that,' Deirdre said.

'And also, maybe more important, is the way you didn't try and stop anything happening. Another person would have, you know.'

Deirdre did not reply.

'I'm very glad you married Richard. I say that sincerely.'

'That's very nice of you,' Deirdre looked at her directly.

★

Before her mother died the old lady had wanted to see Richard and Deirdre and they had gone to London together. Her mother, too, had agreed with Katherine – Richard was lucky to have married Deirdre, luckier than either his father or grandfather had been with their wives. Her mother was dead a year. She had left her jewellery to Clare just as she had promised and left nothing else at all.

*

There were days when Katherine had no idea what to do. Days when the paint did nothing, when she knew there would be no point in going into the studio at night to develop the ideas she had worked on during the day. She had to learn to let herself rest and stay calm. She had to keep looking, keep watching the river, just concentrate on that. And a few times late at night, she left her flat in the converted outhouse and went back to her studio and turned on all the lights – she then would take out everything she had done, all the plans, notes, sketches and the big canvases, and she would look, and walk around the studio. There would be no sound.

She tried to empty her mind, to let nothing in apart from seeing what was in front of her. No ideas, no memories, no thoughts. Just the things around her.

Three or four times like this the break came. There was a way. Any mark on the canvas would be a way. A random stroke, meaning nothing, pointing towards nothing. Any colour, any shape. There must be no doubts. Thus in the small hours paintings came into being.

The valley in red and brown, not as though it were autumn and the red and brown were the colours of the

229

trees, but as though it were winter in red and brown. Dusk on the Slaney in winter in red and brown. The river of small pools and currents.

The valley as though painted from beneath, as though it were a map. The curve in the Slaney snaking across the painting in every colour to re-create the water, the sky in the water and the river bed underneath. And then there was the land around, the way it had been tilled, the farmed ground. And the house her father built during the Troubles. And everywhere the sun pouring down light on the world.

The Road to Dublin

On the road to Dublin. April. Michael Graves lit a cigarette for Katherine and handed it to her.

'Why don't you learn to drive?' she asked him.

'I'm too old.'

'You're too contrary.'

'I'm too contrary.'

'Sometimes I become tired driving. My back hurts.'

'You're too contrary,' he laughed.

'I'm too old,' she said, 'that's why my back hurts. We're both too old. That's why I wish you could drive.'

'I wish I was a maid again,' he sang. 'But a maid again I never will be till cherries grow on an ivy tree.'

It was two weeks since all the paintings had been delivered to the gallery in Dublin. Sixteen of the large canvases were ready and framed. These paintings would fill the two rooms upstairs in the gallery. Down in the return they could hang some of the watercolours from Ballyconnigar: the small modest images of sand, sea and sky, muted, almost colourless. They made no statement, they tried nothing new, nobody could dislike them. They were competent; they had ease.

The other work was bigger and more risky. Her

chances of success were slim. She had not seen the work framed and hanging in the gallery. She had left others to arrange her work.

'I'm nervous,' she said. 'Do you remember the way Miguel used to be? I feel just like that. The week before an exhibition, Miguel always reminded me of a dog looking for a place to hide a bone, even if he had only one painting in the show. He could not keep still. You were never like that.'

'I never put so much of myself into a painting as either Miguel or you did. I only used to worry about what would sell,' he said.

'I've put so much into these paintings, I'm not sure if I've anything left. I've exhausted myself. Maybe I should have left something over.'

Gorey, Arklow. Now the sky was completely clear. For weeks there had been nothing to do. Odd memories trickling in and Miguel back on her mind, preying on her, almost talking to her sometimes. She spoke to Richard about it one day, and once the subject was opened, they discussed it over and over. Sometimes if they had talked at lunchtime and he had to go, he would come back that evening with questions. He wanted to know when things happened, did this happen before or after this, what year was that, what were the results and consequences of various actions? Katherine left out her feelings, she told him what happened, where they had gone, what they had done, what Miguel had said, what he looked like, anecdotes, unconnected events, days. Later, he wanted her to fill these in, to add in the feeling, the colour. Did you love him then? he would ask. Or how did you feel when that happened? Or what did you think then? And these were the difficult questions.

'It's going to be a great day. You'll be swimming soon,' Michael Graves said. They drove through Rathnew.

'Not today though,' she said. 'I'm afraid to go and look at the paintings. I'm not afraid of the opening. That will be bearable. There will be people I'll have to talk to. The gallery will be full of people. I won't know any of them and that will be even better. And there will be all that wine. No, it's seeing the paintings I'm afraid of.'

'Have a drink first,' he said.

'I don't know. That might make things worse.'

Newtown Mount Kennedy. Bray. Richard and Deirdre would drive along the same road later for the opening. They had never been to one before. She was glad when they said they would not stay long; she did not want to be responsible for anyone else. She had herself and Michael to look after.

'What do you want to do?' she asked.

'You mean today?'

'Yes.'

'Whatever you want to do.'

'I want you to come to the gallery with me now.'

'Okay.'

'I want you to have lunch with me.'

'Okay.'

'Then I'll go home and I'll meet you in the gallery later on. I'll have to wash and change.'

She parked in Nassau Street and they went around the corner to the gallery. It was nearing lunchtime, the streets were filling up. She went into the gallery in Dawson

Street feeling that she was waiting for news: what would they look like? It was easy downstairs, as she knew it would be, to look at the watercolours.

'You'll have no trouble selling these anyway. If I'd money I'd buy one myself,' Michael said.

The front room of the Taylor Gallery had six of the large paintings. What amazed her seeing them again was the thickness of the paint, how much work each painting contained, how many decisions she had made, working over and over each new change on the canvas in a way that would be impossible to repeat. And yet some strokes had been left there without any work.

The paintings took over the room; each was the same size and depicting more or less the same landscape. But the colours were different; there was simply a mood and shape to each painting, a sense of a river flowing through well-cultivated land, a sense of similar horizons that illustrated the same place.

The effect in the back room was even stronger.

'What do you think?' she turned to Michael.

'I think they're good,' he said and smiled.

'Let's go before anyone sees us,' she said.

They walked back along Nassau Street towards Lincoln Place.

*

'We haven't seen you for a long time,' the waitress said when they went into Bernardo's.

'You do have a table, don't you?' Katherine asked.

The waitress pointed to a table against the wall and they sat down.

'Here we are again,' Michael said. 'What are we going to have?'

The waitress came over and Katherine ordered.

After the meal they had liqueurs and coffee. They walked back to the car.

'I'll see you later,' she said.

She drove down the quays to Blackhall Place and turned up towards home.

*

The silence in the house. It struck her as she closed the door that there would be silence in the house. She put her back against the door and listened. This was what she had gained: an appreciation of the subtleties of silence, a calm joy each time she came in the door that there would be silence. She went upstairs and took off her clothes in the back bedroom and put on her dressing-gown and slippers. There was time to sit around for the afternoon, have a bath, listen to a record, think. She got some orange juice from the fridge. She lay back on the couch with a cushion under her head.

It must have been March when they first arrived in Llavorsi. Even in the early afternoon the air had been freezing and sharp, like no air she had ever breathed before and the stream was swollen with ice just melted. It had resembled some point near the edge of the world after seven punishing hours on the bus from Barcelona, up and up, twists in the foothills of the Pyrenees. It was noon when they reached the summit after an hour's even steeper climb and she had seen the valley down below for the first time, fertile like a promised land.

235

She was afraid that day to touch Miguel or talk to him. It had been so fraught between them on the journey, it reminded her of the air in Barcelona when it became purple before a thunderstorm: a fierce tension while you waited for the rain. It reminded her of travel, of being in a strange place for the first day, walking the streets of London, Paris, Barcelona.

It reminded her of mornings in Barcelona when she'd had no sleep, or two hours' sleep and all she wanted was some small physical contact before falling into a day's weak sleep.

Her mind began to wander to the time before Richard was born, just after she was married, and it was the summer, one of those high, rich, summer days in Enniscorthy. For some reason she had had no sleep and it was early, maybe ten or half ten in the morning. She walked across the fields looking for Tom; at first her search was casual, almost indifferent, but as she proceeded and was unable to find him she became more concerned and almost frantic. There was the smell of warm grass that day, all these years later she could still smell the warm grass. When she found him, she could not explain. She called him from the gate where he was standing with some workmen.

'I want to talk to you.'

'Now?'

'Come back to the house with me. I want to talk to you.'

'There are things to be done here. Not now.'

'You must come now. You must come now. You must come now,' she had pleaded.

He asked her what it was, but she insisted he come back with her and she would tell him.

'Come upstairs,' she said.

'What is it?' he asked and smiled, as though puzzled.

She came towards him; she was almost unable to breathe.

'It's twelve o'clock in the morning,' he said.

'I want to make love,' she said.

He turned away from her and began to unbutton his shirt. The whiteness of his bare back was made more noticeable by his red arms and neck. She was already naked behind him. She put her hands on her own breasts and held them. The silence between them was only broken by her breathing; he stood still for a moment when he was naked and she moved towards him and put her arms around him. After a few moments she grasped his hand and brought him to the bed. He seemed heavier, fleshier in the morning light. When she took his penis in her hand and held it he gasped for a second and his hands seemed to tighten on her back as though she was hurting him. He lay on top of her and stopped her when she tried to push his penis into her. He lay on top of her without entering her and kissed her slowly on the mouth. She detected an anxiety in him, a sort of weariness, but there was still something forcing him to go on. She kept her hand down between her legs, massaging herself with her fingers, doing what he would never do for her. After a while he came into her and moved his hands along her breasts as he began to push in and out. One hand she kept down on herself and the other she held at his neck. When he began to ejaculate she heard him breathing faster and whimper for a moment as though he were in pain. Her orgasm came after his and she began to cry out as though she was having a fit.

'Don't make noise,' he said to her. 'Don't make noise.'

He put on his clothes quietly as though it was the early morning and he didn't want to wake her. She didn't look up when he touched her on the shoulder for a moment before he left the room. He left her to fall into a long, satisfying sleep. But for days afterwards he avoided being in the bedroom when she was there and at night kept to his side of the bed; he seemed afraid of her.

*

Over the mantelpiece now in her house in Dublin hung *The Hammock*, the painting she had bought from Ramon Rogent almost thirty years before. Her old teacher; she had kept the painting with her to remember him and his studio in Puertaferrisa. There was still a power in the painting which she had not observed for many years, how he had traced the twine of the hammock using every colour under the sun: yellow, pink, red, black, white. And the intricate, colourful designs on the woman's dress and the hill behind. But governing everything was the hard light of Majorca, harder than anything in Catalonia, the soul taken out of every colour and just its dead, hard body left glinting like granite.

Ramon was dead; and Tom; and Miguel. And this was an ordinary day among the days she had been allotted during the time she would be alive, a day when they would all live with her, old ghosts.

She phoned for a taxi to take her to the gallery when she had had her bath and dressed herself. Dublin was quiet; the quay was deserted.

John Taylor, who ran the gallery, introduced her to the man who was to make the speech, the man from the Arts Council. He was much younger than she had imagined.

'Did you come up from Enniscorthy this morning?' he asked her.

'Yes, we drove up.'

'Do you often come to Dublin?'

'I live in Dublin,' she said and noticed that the man's attention seemed to have focused on someone else who had just entered. She excused herself and walked into the back room and found Michael Graves.

'Do you know any of these people?' she asked him.

'No,' he whispered.

'Let's go and have a drink, we can come back,' she said.

'You can't do that.'

'I can. I think I'm going to be sick.'

'Are you all right?' He stood beside her and helped her to stand and lean against the wall.

'I think I'm fine.' She put her hands to her face. 'I feel awful,' she said.

'You go down,' she said. 'See if Richard and Deirdre are here.'

When he had gone she stayed there, leaning against the wall. She could hear her blood thundering in her head.

A man came towards her in the gallery and shook her hand. 'Delighted to see you again,' he said. She smiled. Several people turned to look at her as she moved across the gallery which was now filling up, to where Michael stood with Richard and Deirdre. John Taylor brought her a chair and a glass of water.

The man from the Arts Council was introduced and began to speak.

'What's his name?' Deirdre whispered to her.

'I don't know. I think it's in Irish,' Katherine said. 'An Irish name.'

He spoke for some time about Ireland and Spain, he ended by talking about her skill and brilliance. She approached him when he had finished and thanked him.

Michael introduced her to a critic from one of the Sunday newspapers who wanted to meet her.

'Do you know all these people?' Her tone was sharper than she meant it to be.

'Yes, I suppose I do,' he said.

'Who are they all? What do they do?'

'Didn't you invite them?'

'No, the gallery did. I don't have any objection to them. I just want you to tell me who they are.'

'Some of them are painters, some are buyers, others just go to openings all the time; they enjoy them.'

'Isn't that interesting?' Katherine said and looked at Michael.

*

They went with Richard and Deirdre to the Royal Hibernian Hotel, had a drink there and then said goodbye on the steps. Michael said he wanted to go to Larry Tobin's pub in Duke Street.

'Am I going to be a millionaire?' Katherine asked John Taylor, when they were seated in the pub.

'The watercolours were going fast,' he said.

'And not the paintings?'

'Not yet anyway.'

They were joined in the pub by a number of people she had met with Michael before. They talked about her exhibition.

By ten o'clock she wanted to leave, but the conversations kept on around her; more people joined them and others went away; more brandy appeared in front of her each time she wanted to go.

'Michael, I'm going this time. I can't stay on drinking.'

'No, just hold on.'

'I haven't eaten.'

'I'll get you a sandwich,' he went up to the bar and came back with a ham sandwich and some mustard.

'I'm going to go home soon. I really am.'

*

They stood together out on the street.

'I'll walk up towards the Green with you. I'll get a taxi.'

'Do you want to go and eat?'

'No, I want to go home. Ring me tomorrow. I'm exhausted.'

'I hate going home on my own,' he said.

'I'll see you in the morning.'

'Your exhibition was very good.'

She sighed.

'But it's past now, isn't it? I've to do more work now.'

She got into a taxi and pulled down the window.

'Why don't you come over in the morning and we'll have breakfast.'

He smiled and walked away.

At the bottom of Grafton Street she told the taxi driver to stop. She handed him two pounds and told him she was sorry but she wanted to walk. It was a fine night. There were crowds in Westmoreland Street going to a disco. She walked down the river and crossed at the Halfpenny Bridge. Down the river at night when there were no cars coming the only sound was the tapping of rope against the flagpoles. A few alarm bells were ringing down the quays and the blare of an ambulance could be heard in the background. She looked down into the water, the ink-black water, and across the river at Adam and Eve's opposite the Four Courts. By now Michael Graves would be putting the key in the door of his flat in Hatch Street, facing into another night.

She turned into Blackhall Place and walked up past the Incorporated Law Society towards Manor Street. She walked up Aughrim Street. The clouds were passing quickly across the full moon. The full moon shining over the Phoenix Park.

When she came to the bottom of Carnew Street she hesitated as she saw there was a figure sitting at her doorstep. She stood for a moment wondering if she should alert a neighbour until she realised who it was.

'I thought you were a ghost,' she smiled. 'What are you doing here?'

Michael Graves stood up. 'Where were you? I thought I was going to have to sit here all night. I got a taxi over here.'

'I walked, but I didn't expect to see you. I was thinking about you.'

She opened the door and turned on the light in the front room.

'Schubert,' he said.

'What Schubert?'

'There's one you always play.'

'Hold on. I'll get a drink first. What do you want? Whiskey, brandy, gin, Harp?'

'Let's have a gin and tonic each, lots of ice.'

'The fire's set, you can put a match to it.'

When Katherine came back into the room with a tall glass of gin and tonic for each of them, Michael had drawn the curtains and switched on a lamp. He was looking at Ramon Rogent's painting over the mantelpiece.

'This is perfect,' she said.

He settled himself in an armchair and, when she had put the needle on the record, she sat on a stool beside him.

'The gin,' he said. 'The taste reminds me of things.'

He left silence as the music soared; when she rose to turn the sound down he spoke again.

'Things.' He almost whispered the word.

She glanced at him as he clinked the ice around in the glass.

'We've come as far as this,' she said. 'I suppose we should be grateful.'

'Maybe,' he said and smiled softly. 'Maybe.'

She stared into the fire as it began to flare, then turned and looked at him.

'I'm glad you came back here tonight,' she said, 'and I will make up a bed for you when the record ends. And then I'll go to bed myself. I'm tired. Maybe we will light the fire again tomorrow if it's cold. That would be something. Maybe we won't do much tomorrow.'

'I'll stay up for a while,' he said. 'It's nice being here.'

They listened to the music as it became intense. Soon the slow movement began. She wished for something else now, some time in the past or something that might have been different, but soon she stopped herself thinking. She closed her eyes and kept them closed until the movement came to an end, and then she stood up and slowly began to get ready for the night.

Michael did not stir. He sipped his drink and then turned and smiled at her when she came back into the room with the fireguard which she put in front of the fire. When his bed was ready, she came and told him; and then she made her own way upstairs. She would, she knew, be fast asleep before he moved from the chair.

Afterword

The journey due south from Dublin by train is beautiful. Beyond Dun Laoghaire, the train line cuts through rock overlooking the sea. Several times as it emerges from tunnels it seems perched right over the water. And then, beyond Bray, the scene becomes gentler. For some miles, the train runs by a short stony strand with the calm Irish Sea on one side. At Wicklow it moves inland, and then a few miles north of the town of Enniscorthy it begins to follow the line of the river Slaney, the river which Edmund Spenser called in *The Faerie Queen* 'the sandy Slane'.

Spenser in the 1580s passed through the town; indeed he held a lease on Enniscorthy and the land around for a short period before selling it on. One of his closest friends, the poet Lodovick Bryskett, however, stayed in the town for many years and wrote letters to London making clear that he was living in a dangerous borderland, a place where English civility was fragile, where the barbarous natives represented a constant danger to the new English who had taken vast tracts of territory in the name of the Queen. The Slaney valley contained rich land, and over the next century most of it changed hands, the native Irish, or those who had begun to behave like natives, being forced into more boggy or hilly terrain. All along the valley, on both sides of the river, are the beautiful old houses of the planters, people with name like Deacon and Proctor, some in ruins, but many of them still intact and stately.

On Sundays when I was growing up we used to go for drives through this landscape either in the small family car or in my aunt's car. As children, we were as interested in where the best ice-cream could be had as we were in stories about history and ancient conflicts. Sometimes, however, my uncle, who had fought in the War of Independence, would point to an old house and mention that he had, as a young insurgent, raided it for guns in 1920 or 1921. I remember one house because he remarked on his luck to find freshly cooked chickens during the raid; they were delicious, he said. By listening only half the time, I picked up a considerable amount of information about big houses around Enniscorthy which were burned or raided and the reasons why. Thus I knew that the Irish novelist Molly Keane was Captain Skrine's daughter, and that the burning of her house when she was a child had been done by my uncle or some of his associates. I did not read her novel *Two Days in Aragon* about this event, however, or know it existed, until I had written my own novel *The South*. But on meeting her in 1981, as I was planning my novel, I took a long and close look at her – she was born in 1905 – and I found that encounter very useful as I worked on my book.

There is another encounter which might have mattered more. It is all the more powerful and present because I am less sure about it. Between 1978, when I came back to Ireland from Spain, and the mid-1980s, I would travel to Enniscorthy some weekends, taking the train from Dublin on a Friday evening. For the first hour, the train would be full of commuters, but then, beyond Wicklow, the numbers would thin out; it would be easy from the accents to tell the difference between people from Arklow, Gorey, Enniscorthy and Wexford, even though these towns were between ten and twenty miles away from each other. Also, I would know a good number of the people from Enniscorthy by name, or by sight.

On one of those Fridays some time in 1979 a woman got on the train at one of the stations outside Dublin and travelled south. She sat on the side away from the sea in the last seat of a carriage. I had a very clear view of her. She was not dressed like the normal travellers on this train; she was wearing worn but expensive tweed, and good shoes; she seemed deeply preoccupied and was travelling alone. She looked grander and richer than we were, the rest of the travellers, and in the casual shorthand of the time, I might have surmised that she was a Protestant. By this I mean that there was a sense of old stability, old money about her. While she did not appear arrogant or anything like that, she did, however, seem formidable, someone not easily frightened. She stood out, since people like that did not usually travel on this train.

I got off at Enniscorthy, and in my dreams, or maybe in reality (I am not sure about this part), there was someone to meet the woman I had seen on the train at the station, as there would be in the novel *The South* whose contours began to grow in my imagination. She would become Katherine Proctor; this journey, the journey I saw her on, would be her first journey home in many years. This landscape is the landscape of the south, the south of

Ireland, in a country often known in political parlance as 'The South', as opposed to 'The North'; Katherine, having left this place, had journeyed to Spain, to the warm south.

I knew exactly where she had been, even though her journey to Catalonia in Spain had been a quarter of a century before mine. I had gone to Barcelona on 24 September 1975 when I was twenty. I had stayed first in an old pension on the corner of Carrer del Pi and Carrer de la Portaferrissa. The city then almost belonged to the 1950s. No tourists came to Barcelona; they went to the coast rather than the city. The shops were old-fashioned. There was a great sense of custom and decorum in the streets. There were also police in the streets, and people were afraid of the police, and this gave private life a greater intensity, as it did friendships and family relations. When Franco died on 20 November 1975, things began to change, but no one was clear in the first year or two what that change was going to be.

I worked as a teacher of English. One of my students was in her sixties. She was a Catalan woman of great charm and intelligence who lived near the church of Santa Maria del Mar. She had studied Catalan in the 1930s with the great lexicographer Pompeu Fabra. She had seen Casals play in Prades in the French Pyrenees when he came there after the Civil War, and maybe also before the war in the Palau de la Musica, the city's splendid concert hall. I began to go to the concerts in the Palau, especially on Saturday evenings, and I began to study Catalan as well as Spanish, and I started to ask anyone I could find about the war, about what had happened in the city between 1936 and 1939 and in the years of repression afterwards.

While the Picasso Museum and the Miró Foundation were open then, and I was aware of what these two painters had meant for the city, and how many years they had lived elsewhere, there was another museum which began to interest me almost more. It was in the building in the Parc de la Ciutadella which now houses the Catalan parliament; it showed the work of the Catalan painters who went to Paris only once or twice and who had then come home. I became fascinated by the work of two of them especially – Isidre Nonell (1872–1911) and Joaquin Mir (1873–1940), contemporaries of Picasso's who had continued to paint in a style they had learned in their twenties. Later, as the novel was taking shape I became interested in the Catalan painter Ramón Rogent (1920–1958), and I put him as a real character into the book and allowed Katherine to study art with him and buy *The Hammock* from him, one of his best works.

In the three years that I lived in Barcelona I often went to a small village in the Pyrenees called Farrera de Pallars. The journey there, by bus, was then even more spectacular than it is now; the roads have been improved and some tunnels built. The village is on the side of the hill, each stone house with slated roof poised to get maximum sunlight. There was no shop or bar, and many of the old houses were vacant or abandoned. Sometimes, in the evening, I would go and have a beer in the house where there was a public telephone and listen to talk about the village in the past, about the families who had lived in the houses, and about what had happened in the war when the village was taken twice, first by the Loyalists, or the Reds as they were often called, and then by Franco's forces. Out of the village there were many old paths, some of them havens for smugglers, since the village was close to Andorra.

This village, and the magnificent landscape around, the snow that came in the winter and stayed for months, the beautiful high sky in the summer, were a revelation. Being there was pure excitement, as the city of Barcelona and the colours of the Mediterranean were pure excitement. This grew more intense as the plans for a new and democratic Spain and an autonomous Catalonia became clear.

Once I was back in Ireland, however, Spain became something I had lost. I missed almost every aspect of it, as I had missed Ireland in my early months in Barcelona. I was aware that the Slaney valley had been colonized and fought over, much as the Catalan landscape had. But no one, as far as I knew, had made paintings of the Blackstairs mountains in Wexford, or the light over the Slaney at certain times of the year. There was no Irish Picasso or Miró, and no Wexford version of Nonell, or Mir, or Rogent that I had paid any real attention to. Ireland, despite its literary heritage, was, in many respects, a strange dull backwater, or so it seemed to me in 1978, as I tried to find work in Dublin.

The city lacked colour and it was out of this lack that the novel began to take shape. I slowly became aware of a number of painters who had indeed worked with the Irish landscape. They had a real glamour and independence of mind all the more apparent because of the general drabness around them. Many of them had lived in France or in Spain. Slowly, I began to look at art made by an earlier generation of Irish woman painters such as Norah McGuinness (1901–1980), Mary Swanzy (1882–1978), Mainie Jellett (1897–1944) and Evie Hone (1894–1955).

As I started to work as a journalist I could meet at openings artists such as Anne Yeats (1919–2001) and younger painters such as Camille Souter, Anne Madden and Maria Simmonds-Gooding, women painters who worked in France or in the west of Ireland, and came to Dublin merely for exhibition openings. There was glamour, mystery and singularity about them. They seemed made for a novelist in search of a protagonist who was an artist.

There were also a number of men, whose backgrounds were close to my small-town, Catholic background, who had become painters. I had known Paul Funge, for example, since the early 1970s. His paintings of Spain and the edges of towns in county Wexford began to interest me, as much as the freedom in his spirit did. Other painters, such as Patrick Collins, who had lived in France and painted the landscape of Sligo, or Tony O'Malley, who had made drawings of paintings of the Wexford landscape in the 1940s, and suffered from tuberculosis and then lived in St Ives in Cornwall, or Sean McSweeney, who painted in Wicklow and then in Sligo, or Brian Bourke, who lived in Galway, began to fascinate me. These were figures who worked to create or re-create Irish light in paint; they had no interest in international fame or trends in the art market. I began to see them as examples of how to live in Ireland, and they made their way also into the fabric of my novel as I imagined the figure of Michael Graves.

The problem I had was the problem any novelist faces – when to begin, how to begin. As the characters became real for me, as the outline of what would happen in the book became apparent, as a sense of its tone and style took shape, I began to get more work as a journalist and as an editor. With one chapter of the book written – a chapter I later abandoned – I went to work in late 1982 as editor of Ireland's main current affairs magazine. This was not an ideal job for a novelist. It took up most of my waking time. The novel lived on in my dream time. I was doing everything to it except writing it.

One day, as a relief from the tedium of thinking about Irish politics, I went to interview the painter Barrie Cooke. As we stood in front of one of his canvases, I wondered how he could combine what seemed to me like deep deliberation, a sense of line and tone that was fully controlled, and also a swirling energy which gave the paintings a sort of flowing power. He managed the paint and then let it loose, or perhaps did both at the same moment. I wished I was doing that with my novel, rather than sitting in the small office in Merrion Row correcting proofs and controlling budgets. When I asked him how he began a painting, he said something that became useful to me. 'You make a mark,' he said, as he gestured the making of an almost random mark with an imaginary paint-brush.

Sometimes in the evenings and at weekends, living in the top floor of a house in Harcourt Terrace, I would make a mark, using a manual typewriter. Once some chapters had been completed, I began to go on free weekends to the Tyrone Guthrie Centre, a retreat for artists, in Monaghan, close to the border with Northern Ireland. I would work all Friday evening, all day Saturday and then most of Sunday before travelling back to Dublin. If there is a jaggedness and an intensity about the tone and the structure of the novel, it comes from the fact that much of it was written in snatched time.

I remember in the summer of 1984 working on the book in hotel rooms on the Algarve in Portugal, and then in the Metropole Hotel in Lisbon. One day, when I had no idea how to proceed, when no new images came, when I felt I was blocked with the book, I remembered what Barrie Cooke had said. I made a mark. I decided that I would write the first thing that came into my head and then make it stick. What came was: 'The sea. A grey shine on the sea.'

I was surprised by this and began to work with it. I had allowed Katherine to live in an apartment in Barcelona that I had lived in. Her house in the Pyrenees still belongs to my friends Bernard and Mary Loughlin, who had first rented it in the 1970s. In Dublin, I had given her the house in Carnew Street in Stoneybatter which I had bought in 1983 and where I began to live in 1989. I let her live there before I did. But the big house in Wexford where she was from and to which she returned I knew only from the out-side. Now, as I wrote these sentences 'The sea. A grey shine on the sea.' a world that I knew well could be conjured up. It was the stretch of coast between Ballyvaldon and Curracloe on the east coast of County Wexford. We had gone as a family there every summer for many years when I was growing up. Later I discovered that the painter Tony O'Malley had made watercolours and drawings there in the 1940s. It had not occurred to me before that it was a place which could be used for fiction, that I could get something from its modest colours and easy tones. I would come to conjure up that landscape again many times in fiction just as the village in the Pyrenees would appear again in the story 'A Long Winter'.

The chapter, written in Portugal in 1984, called 'The Sea', was published in the *Irish Times* by Caroline Walsh, who was editing a series of stories for the paper. But the novel was not finished. Even when I left the magazine early in 1985 and had time on my hands, it remained two-thirds done. I travelled in South America and Africa and did not work on the book. Slowly, however, in the spring of 1986, I returned to it and finished it, and had another draft done by September 1986.

The problem was then that no one would publish it. Almost every London publisher turned it down. The first one to whom my agent Imogen Parker sent it lost it and did not ask for another copy. One other publisher presumed that I was a woman, and, on turning the book down, wrote: 'If she writes anything else, do let us know.' Imogen one day said to me: 'If it's the last thing I do, I am doing to sell this book.' Two years and two months passed before the book was accepted, by which time I had written my first non-fiction book and had almost finished my second, and I had written the opening of my second novel. I remember that day in London as I was passing through the city on my way from Barcelona to Dublin – it was close to Christmas 1988 – when Imogen told me that she had a publisher for it. Over the next year, with the help of the editor Marsha Rowe at Serpent's Tail, I did a great deal of revision on *The South*, also cutting one chapter and adding another. The book finally appeared in May 1990.

COLM TÓIBÍN
2015

PICADOR CLASSIC
CHANGE YOUR MIND

PICADOR CLASSIC

On 6 October 1972, Picador published its first list of eight paperbacks. It was a list that demonstrated ambition as well as cultural breadth, and included great writing from Latin America (Jorge Luis Borges's *A Personal Anthology*), Europe (Hermann Hesse's *Rosshalde*), America (Richard Brautigan's *Trout Fishing in America*) and Britain (Angela Carter's *Heroes and Villains*). Within a few years, Picador had established itself as one of the pre-eminent publishers of contemporary fiction, non-fiction and poetry.

What defines Picador is the unique nature of each of its authors' voices. The Picador Classic series highlights some of those great voices and brings neglected classics back into print. New introductions - personal recommendations if you will - from writers and public figures illuminate these works, as well as putting them into a wider context. Many of the Picador Classic editions also include afterwords from their authors which provide insight into the background to their original publication, and how that author identifies with their work years on.

Printed on high quality paper stock and with thick cover boards, the Picador Classic series is also a celebration of the physical book.

Whether fiction, journalism, memoir or poetry, Picador Classic represents timeless quality and extraordinary writing from some of the world's greatest voices.

Discover the history of the Picador Classic series and
the stories behind the books themselves at
www.picador.com/classic